Bob Moats

I0567954

Toxic Murders

1

Toxic Murders

For information and address:

Magic 1 Productions

P.O. Box 524, Fraser MI 48026-0524

Website: http://murdernovels.com

Cover by Bob Moats

Bob Moats

Other Jim Richards series books by Bob Moats

For a preview or to purchase a book, go to
http://murdernovels.com

What a few people are saying about Murder Novels by Bob Moats

Mr. Moats, I just got your novel "Classmate Murders" and have to let you know, I read it in one evening. That is the first book I have ever done that with. That was the most enjoyable book I have ever read. I just started reading e-books, and reading again, after getting my wife a Kindle. This book was my 12th, and the best. I just got Las Vegas Showgirls to (read) tomorrow evening. I look forward to reading many of your books in this series. I have been searching for an author and books that were fun, entertaining reads. Your books are just the ticket.

Regards, A new fan, Bill from South Carolina

****

Another very nice comment submitted through my website from Micki P.:

"I recently was given a kindle for my 60th birthday. The first book I downloaded was the Classmate Murders and have now read every one of the them. Today I started on the Fatal Rejection series. Thank you for the wonderful ride with Jim and Penny and all the rest of the troop. I have laughed and giggled thru the stories, my poor family gave me the strangest looks! Now I really want a little Yorkie!! Fatal Rejection so far is another great read! I will be looking out for more of Jim Richards and since you are my #1 Author, anything of yours I can find."

Extra special thanks to:

Special thanks to Val Brooks who edited the first half of this book and to Susan Haughton for finishing it.

Thanks to the beta readers Cindy Gross Valstad and Al Norris for their expert input.

Thank you to all the people who purchased this book. I hope you enjoy it as much as I enjoyed writing it for my faithful readers.

The Jim Richards Family of Readers is listed in the back of the book.

Toxic Murders by Bob Moats

Chapter 1

"I wonder how Jim is going to take this?" Lynn said to her husband, Deacon, as they stood at the front counter of the Richards Investigations office. Lacey was at her desk behind the couple wondering what she was talking about.

"What's going on?" Lacey asked.

"This review of Jim's latest book in the Review-Journal. This woman was vicious and mean." Lynn turned back to Lacey. "I know Jim has endured bad reviews online where he sells his books. But this is being spread to all the people in Vegas who read this newspaper. He may not like that."

"Jim has a tough skin, he'll get over it," Deacon offered.

"I hope so, this review is just brutal. I don't understand, Jim writes non-fiction true crime, about cases we've had in the past. I can see a bad review for a lousy fiction book, I've read a few bad books myself. It's easy to slam a book for having a bad plot, but not a true-to-life story. This woman smeared his book's writing and even his editor. Complaining about the grammar and the way it was written, like a 13 year old girl wrote it." She went back to the paper and read portions, ""Reminded me of Nancy Drew...could have been written by a teenage girl," "Silly," "Makes no sense," "Dialogue is horrible," "Complete boredom," "Story is implausible," "Cheap and nasty," "Absolutely appalling," "One dimensional as if a 13 year old wrote this," "Pedestrian," "A first draft that appears to merit no further effort," "Bad grammar, syntax, punctuation...completely unrealistic characters, pages of pointless 'cute' banter that no one who has ever actually talked to an adult would dare call realistic," and so on. This woman must think she's some big shot reviewer."

"She's not," came a voice from the hallway going to the offices. Jim came out to the lobby and stood holding his copy of the paper. "She's probably some frustrated wannabe reviewer who sent the review to the editor of the entertainment section and he had the balls to print it. I'm not even bothering with giving him a hard time, it's useless to respond to rude people. I'll just murder her in my next book."

"Jim, you write true crime, so you'd have to actually murder her to include her in a book," Deacon said.

"I guess I have a problem then." Jim smiled and went to the counter, putting his paper down on it. "I'll just ignore this and it'll go away. Not a lot of people who live in Vegas buy my books. Mostly people from other places wanting to know what goes on crime-wise in Sin City."

"What kind of crap is this?" Penny exclaimed as she came in the front door, holding a copy of the paper. "I was given this at the studio after I taped my show. The intern asked if this was about my husband when he gave it to me." She went to Jim, "Bad enough you get bad reviews on Amazon, but not here in the city that you protect."

Jim was holding in a laugh. "You could murder the woman, then I can write about it," he said.

"I just may, if I can find her. But these inconsiderate people hide behind their writings, using a nickname. This one called herself, Mrs. Repas. I'm sure it's a fake name." Penny turned and kissed Jim, then she turned to Deacon. "So Deacon, how do you like working for Jim now that you quit LVPD?"

"I'm happy, although Captain Weber isn't. I think he was about to have a stroke when I turned in my walking papers. He said, first Lynn left, now me. I think he was worried he'd have to work now without us around to investigate cases."

They all looked towards the front entrance as a woman about seventy entered the lobby. She stopped after seeing all the people in the lobby, and looked confused. Jim went to her.

"Can I help you?" he asked.

"I need some protection. I understand you have people to bodyguard a person," she replied.

"We do that service, and you are?" Jim asked.

"I'm Virginia Repas and I have a stalker."

Penny's head snapped around when she heard the name. She went to the woman and asked, "Are you the woman who wrote a review about a book called the Lipstick Murders?"

The woman looked shocked. "Yes, I did write that, why?"

"Who sent you here?" Penny asked.

"I asked a police officer who took my report about being stalked."

"Do you know who owns this firm?"

"I haven't any idea, what are you getting at?"

She pointed to Jim and said, "This man is the owner, his name is Jim Richards and he wrote the book you slammed. I think it's a little coincidental that you came here."

Now the woman was really surprised. "I didn't know. I'm sorry, I'll go somewhere else."

Jim stopped her and said, "No, stay. If you need help, that's what we're here for. I don't care if you wrote that review, we have a job to do here."

She looked apprehensive, but said she'd stay. Jim turned to Lynn and Deacon and said, "We can provide her with protection, but I think we need to find this stalker. Why don't you two talk to her and see what we can do."

Lynn came forward and said, "Please, follow me." She and Deacon led the woman to Lynn's office, now being shared with Deacon since he started working there.

Penny went to Jim and said, "You're not actually going to help her are you?"

"If she hadn't been the reviewer, we still would be helping her. Now pull your claws back in." Jim kissed her and went back through the hallway to his office. He picked up Willy who was sleeping on his desk and put the tiny dog on the floor. Penny called him from the front and he barreled out of the room. Jim smiled and sat at his desk.

He looked to the door as another dog came running in. It was Henry, Fred's dog. Henry came up to Jim and sat. "What are you up to?" Jim asked the dog.

"Sorry, he got away from me," said Fred, the building's night watchman, janitor and landscaper, as he was coming into the room. Jim reached down and petted the animal.

"It's all right, we have more than two dogs in this building. Speaking of, are Earl and Trapper in their offices?"

"Yes, they're here, but they're in the lounge relaxing," Fred replied.

Jim stood and picked up Henry. He handed the dog to Fred and started to go out of the room, but stopped. "Did you need me for something?" he asked Fred.

"Nope, I was chasing Henry. I wanted to take him outside."

"Okay, do that and we'll talk later." Jim went down the hall to the door of the next hallway going to the lounge, beside Lynn and Deacon's office. He entered and saw Earl and Trapper sitting at the table eating from bags of Carl's Jr. "You didn't take orders for lunch, how rude."

"You weren't here, and Lynn, Deacon and Lacey weren't hungry."

"Fine. Do you have any cases?"

Earl spoke first, "I got a missing person to find."

"I get to follow a cheating spouse. Really exciting stuff," Trapper said, with a big grin.

"Well, don't eat too much junk food, or you'll get lazy," Jim said with a grin. He went out and over to Lynn's door. It was open and he looked in. Lynn was at her desk talking to the woman as Deacon sat back at his desk, listening. Deacon waved to Jim standing at the door opening. Jim stood listening to them talking as the woman explained what transpired with her stalker.

Jim turned away and went forward towards the lobby again. He was feeling bored since the firm had more than enough investigators with Deacon now a member. After Deacon was nearly killed in his last police case, he wanted to get away from the dangers of being a cop. He wanted to live for his wife and little girl. So he talked to Jim and asked if he could join the firm. Now the roster of investigators was full, so Jim didn't have to work as hard.

He thought many times of retiring and taking his motorhome van to travel the country, if Penny could get the time off of her show. He doubted that she would quit her show, she was having too much fun.

He went through the door to the lobby and found Penny and Lacey reading the newspaper at the counter.

"I'm still not forgiving this woman for this review," Penny said looking up. "I may have to put a hit out on her."

*

Chapter 2

"Leave her alone, she's an old fool of a woman and figures her reviews will make her look important. I'm not the only person she's given bad reviews to. I was listening to her in Lynn and Deacon's office and I understand that one of the authors she slammed has made threats against her. Life threatening threats."

"Threatening threats. Isn't that overkill? Wouldn't using one threat work as well as two?" Penny asked.

"What, are you the grammar police now? You know what I mean," Jim said with a smile. "This woman sounds a bit off in the head. I feel sorry for her, yet I don't like her. She's mean spirited."

"You don't like her? I thought you liked everyone."

"I don't like killers and other such criminals," Jim replied.

"You don't like bad reviews, either," Lacey added.

Jim laughed and said, "No, I don't." He looked at Penny, "Authors depend on good reviews to help bolster sales of their books. If they get bad reviews, then readers will take too much in what a reviewer says and won't buy the book. If a writer isn't selling books, he or she may feel it's useless to continue. Even if the author has a good series of books. Bad reviews can hurt, even if the author doesn't admit it. It's like calling your children ugly."

"So, your books sell well, even with a bad review," Penny said, putting the newspaper down.

"I'm fortunate enough to be established now, and my publisher works hard to promote the books. That's important to have backing. Besides, I have enough money in the bank to cover dry spells in book sales."

"Yes, and I get all that money when you die," Penny said with a laugh.

"I'll leave it all to Willy," Jim shot back. "Now, I'm hungry, do you want to go eat?"

"I thought you'd never ask. A nice sit down meal would be nice. How about Angelo's?"

"Works for me. Lacey, we'll be out of the office, will you watch Willy for us?"

Penny set the tiny dog on the counter and Lacey reached for him. He gave a look that said he was being abandoned once again. "Sorry, big guy. We'll bring you a nice doggie bag," Jim said to the pup. Willy yipped and wagged his tail. "Food makes you happy, too," Jim said, and petted him.

Penny led the attack into the restaurant as Angelo came to his friends. "Mr. and Mrs. R. Good ta see youse."

Angelo still held on to his old school dialect from being part of a mob family. He tried more than once to improve his way of talking, but he would often slip back into his leg-breaker way of speech. He grew up under three different mob families, so it was not easy to listen to the way they talked and not be affected.

"Angelo, good to see you again. How's business?" Jim asked.

"Never been so good. I wish I had done this years ago," Anglo replied, like a proud father. "I'll seat you at our good table." He led them to the table by the fireplace and pulled Penny's chair out for her, "I'll have the waitress over toot sweet."

Jim laughed at Angelo's corrupted use of the old French term, 'tout de suite', which literally means 'all at once'.

"Angelo, has your family rebounded from the death of your cousin?" Jim asked, referring to the murder of Angelo's cousin by the mob boss who wanted to keep himself out of prison. Unfortunately, Jim and Deacon fouled the plan during the wiseguy murders.

"My Aunt had his body transported back to New Jersey, to be buried in their family cemetery." Angelo waved to a waitress and pointed to the table. "How's Mr. Deacon doing since he was shot by the mook?"

"Deacon is all settled in with our firm. He seems happier to be away from the stress of being with the police. Now he can concentrate on his daughter and wife, yet still be able to investigate crime. Without being shot at," Jim said.

"Jim, you've been shot at numerous times and almost killed a couple of those times. So, how does not being with the police make a difference?" Penny asked.

"Okay, you have a point. But he's a lot safer chasing cheating spouses, which is what he wants to do. I think he's backing off and relaxing now."

The waitress bounced over and smiled. Angelo excused himself and left his friends to order.

They placed their orders and sat making small talk. "You know, the firm is busy with clients, but we have a good number of investigators now, so I don't have to kill myself working hard."

Penny almost spit out the water she was sipping, "You don't work hard? I've never seen you work hard."

"I do to work hard," Jim defended. "I've helped Lynn and Deacon solve a good number of their cases."

"You were just lucky. But I'll give you that, you are a good detective," Penny said.

"Private investigator. Please, it sounds better. So, I was thinking since the firm is running so well, even without me, that we'd take a nice long vacation and go see the country."

Penny sat quietly, Jim waited for her to gather her thoughts. He figured she would bring up her show and how the world couldn't live without her.

"I think it's a good idea," was all she said.

"What about your show?" Jim asked, surprised.

Penny reached over and took Jim's hand, "I'm to the point where I'm starting to get tired of it. I just turned sixty-two and I've been in front of the camera for over ten years. Here in Vegas and back in Michigan. We had fun on your book tour a couple years back, even if we did get involved in a murder. And our vacation up to Washington State, that was fun. Maybe we should go back up there."

"Sure, and we got involved in a murder there and you were kidnapped along with Sarah by the drug cartel. That was fun?"

"Sarah and I bonded. She was a fun woman and I'd love to see her again. Why don't you call them and see what they are up to?"

Jim sat staring at his wife. "Okay, I'll do that. What about your show?"

"I'll talk to Gordy. He won't be happy, but he'll get over it. There's any number of local celebrities who would be more than delighted to host my show. Who knows, I may not come back."

"Fine. I'll call Dave and see what he and Sarah are up to. Call Gordy and get your end started."

Their food came and they ate. Angelo came by one more time before they left to pick up Willy at the office. They entered the back door and went to the front lobby where they found Lacey playing with Willy on her desk.

Jim said, "You grab the dog and I'll be in my office calling Dave." He went out as Penny went to get Willy.

"Who's Dave?" Lacey asked.

"He's a sheriff up in Brinnon, Washington, where we visited just before I started my national show."

"Oh, the sheriff whose wife was kidnapped with you and brought down here to show off some drug."

""That's the one. Jim and I may go on another vacation and visit with them."

"What about your show?" Lacey asked.

"I'm taking time off. I may not come back, who knows."

"What? You'd give up your cushy job and travel with Jim? That's fun?"

"I'd like seeing the country before I get too old to travel. My show has been fun for the last ten years, but it's time to take care of myself. I've always wanted to travel, and with our motorhome, we can."

"Well, we'll miss you," Lacey said and tried to smile.

Jim was in his office and dialing the last number he had for Sheriff Dave Chandler. He waited until he heard a voice answer.

"Sheriff's Office, may I help you?"

"Is Sheriff Chandler working?"

"You got him, how may I help you?"

"Dave, this is Jim Richards. Can you talk?"

"Jim, it's good to hear from you. Are you in need of help?" Dave said with a laugh.

"No, as a matter of fact, Penny and I are thinking of going on another vacation. Do you and Sarah think you could put up with us for a short while?"

"Jim, to be honest, Sarah and I had planned on coming down to Vegas to renew our marriage vows. We got married there before we went out to New York. We didn't spend much time in the city before we moved along. So this time we planned on spending a good week there. It should be better than when we assaulted the bad guys while rescuing our wives."

Jim laughed at the memory of the incident. "When are you coming?"

"Our anniversary is in a week and a half. I was going to call you to warn you we were coming, but you beat me to it."

"I'll warn Penny. I'm sure she'll want to make it a big deal wedding. Hope you are ready for that?"

"We basically eloped, so a nice wedding would make Sarah a happy camper. Don't go to a lot of trouble, just a simple ceremony would be nice."

"Okay, I'll let her know and call you back soon." They finished the call and Jim stood. Penny came in with Willy, before he could go out to see her.

"So, did you talk to Dave?" she asked.

"I did and you are going to love this."

*

Chapter 3

"What!" Penny squealed with delight. "When are they coming? Will I have enough time to plan the wedding? I need to call Shelby Francis, our favorite wedding planner, and have her whip up a couple schemes that I can show Sarah. Oh, my God, this is going to be fun!"

"Penny, dear, calm down. Dave said not to make a big deal out of it," Jim said.

"This is a big deal. When your book editor, Valerie, and her boy toy came all the way from Florida to get married, that was a big deal, too. I don't often get the chance to help with a wedding, so this is special. No Elvis preachers, though. Now, when are they coming?"

"Dave said in a week and a half or so. I'll talk to him before that to get organized," Jim said.

"Won't do. I'll call Sarah tonight and get this started," she replied.

Jim was now worried about what this could develop into, but he figured there was not much he could do. The Kraken was released and Perseus wasn't around to stop it. Maybe the women would work this out and it would be fine.

"What about our vacation?" Jim asked.

"Take your vacation, I'll take mine and spend more time with Sarah. Sorry, sweetie, but the trip will have to wait." Penny was bubbling over with excitement that Jim hadn't seen in a while. He let her have her moment. "I'll get with Lynn and we'll call Shelby to start some plans." Penny turned and went out of the room, leaving Willy on the desk looking confused.

"Sorry, buddy, she has a new agenda. Us males will be on the back burner until Dave and Sarah go off on their honeymoon." Jim picked up the dog and went out of his office. He went to the lobby and found Deacon standing at the front entrance talking to the reviewer woman. Jim waited behind him.

The woman left the building and Deacon turned to Jim. "That woman is a psycho. She really believes someone is out to kill her because of a bad review. I'm sure you'd like to murder a few reviewers. But I said, like, not actually."

"No, I wouldn't do that. So, does she have a case?"

"Well, Lynn is going to investigate the author who threatened her and see what she can find. It's probably nothing, but just to be on the safe side we'll check it out. What's up with Penny? She grabbed Lynn and took her back to our office."

"Do you remember Sheriff Dave Chandler and his wife Sarah, from Brinnon, Washington?"

"I do," he replied.

"Well, they are coming to Vegas to re-new their wedding vows and Penny wants to turn it into a big fancy deal."

"Well, I'm sure Lynn will be up for that. She still talks about our wedding."

Jim and Deacon turned to the entrance door when it opened and in came Greg Warren, a detective from Deacon and Lynn's old squad.

"Greg! Good to see you. How's everything back at the precinct?" Deacon asked.

"It's a mess since you left. Can we talk privately? Both you and Jim."

"Sure, follow me." Deacon led them to his office, but stopped at the door. "Uh, Penny and

21

Lynn are in there bouncing around. Jim, can we use your office?"

"Follow me, boys." Jim led them around to his office and put Willy on the desk. Deacon and Greg sat.

"What's up, Greg?" Deacon asked, once Jim had closed the door and sat behind his desk.

"Things have changed since you left. I figured I would be in line for your Lieutenant slot, but it didn't happen. They brought in some hotshot detective from North Vegas PD and he's a real dickhead."

"Who is it, do I know him?" Deacon asked.

"Harvey Boering," Warren replied.

"Boring Boering? They put him in my place?" Deacon said, sounding annoyed.

"Yeah, and he's stirring up the squad by moving people around on cases. I pulled a case of domestic assault. There was no homicide involved. Why? He said it could develop into a homicide, if we sat on it too long. Nip it in the bud, he said. Deacon, you know that we don't have time to follow up on domestic assaults, they usually go away. Sure, sometimes there's a murder, but not often once we face the perp and warn him we will be watching."

"I know, Greg. What did Captain Weber say?"

"He had to bring in Boering, he was ordered to, so he defends the man. It's not a happy squad like when you and Lynn were there."

"Yes, and I left that life behind. I'm sorry for the men who had to stay, but it was my time to get out. You've been there for a long time, can't you retire?"

"Not for another year. If I left now, my pension wouldn't be enough to live on. So I'll stay until I get shot or die from a heart attack."

"I wish we could fit you in here, Greg," Jim spoke, "But we have our fill of investigators."

"No, Jim. If I leave the LVPD, it won't be to get back into investigating. Maybe I'll go into private security for one of the big casinos in town. Tossing drunks and card cheats out of the building. It would be a welcome change."

Deacon smiled, "Don't give up just yet, another year and you can retire on full pension. So, did you come here to tell us about the changes in the precinct?"

"That, and I wanted to tell you about a woman whose husband is missing."

"Isn't missing persons going to take it?" Deacon asked.

"That's what Boering said, just before he ordered me to forget about it. He left the squad to go suck up to Weber while I talked to the woman. She was really worried, hadn't seen him in two days. She said he had problems with gambling and was worried he was in trouble."

"Half the men in this city have trouble with gambling," Jim said.

"True, but she said he goes through a bookie and not the sports book in the casinos."

"Not a smart thing to do," Deacon said. "Did she say who the bookie was?"

"She said she overheard her husband on the telephone and he referred to the guy as Luther . The day her husband disappeared, some men came to the house asking for him. The wife told them he was at work and they left. She said they didn't look friendly. She never saw her husband again." Warren paused, "I would explain all this to Boering, but I know he won't care. He wants our closing rates to look good."

"We had good closings when I was there. Does he expect 100 percent solved cases?"

"That's Boering for you. Mr. Perfect. So I have the name of the wife, if you happen to know of anyone who cares?"

Deacon looked at Jim and they both grinned. "Can't hurt to just talk to her," Deacon said.

"My vacation has been put on hold, so I've got some time," Jim replied. He held out a notepad and told Warren to write down anything he had on the woman. Warren took the pad and started writing.

"I hope this leads to something I can throw in Boering's face. I hate his cocky smile," Warren said.

"We'll keep it between us if we find anything," Deacon said as he took the notepad back and read it.

"Thanks, guys. I'm still steamed that I didn't get the lieutenant slot and they brought in Boering to fill it. I don't think Weber has anything against me, he just wants things to run smoothly, so he doesn't have to work hard."

"I've never known Weber to work hard," Deacon said. "Hang in there, Greg, I think Weber has a year to go before he can retire, too. I'm sure he'll be out as fast as possible."

"Yeah, I know. It's still going to be hell putting up with him and Boering. You and Lynn were the glue that held us together. Williams is still a screw-up. He tries, but never seems to get it right. The rest of the squad is all grumbling about Boering. There's so much dissent that I'm surprised we get anything done."

"Let Jim and me find out if there's more to your missing man and we'll let you take credit if it is something bigger. Maybe Weber will give you some respect."

"Sure, you do all the work and I get the credit. If I wasn't worried about Boering finding out, I'd investigate with you."

"Just let us get to the heart of the matter, then you can take lead on it. It's your case, as long as there is a case," Deacon said.

"Thanks, Deacon. It's hard not having you around for the humor in our miserable days."

"That's me, class clown. Lynn thinks I'm a riot. I guess that's why she's still with me," Deacon said with a big grin.

Warren stood. "Well, I'd better get back before Boering is screaming for me. I'm on my lunch break and he doesn't want us taking more than we need. He says there's crime waiting for us out there."

"Sounds like the only crime is Boering," Jim spoke, as they all stood.

"Thanks again, guys. I appreciate it." He turned to the door with a slight frown and left the room.

Deacon turned to Jim, "Greg has always been a good cop. He's done a lot more than the rest of the squad put together. I hated to leave him, but life goes on."

"So let's find out about the missing husband and see if we can help him."

"You got it, boss."

*

Chapter 4

Penny was feeling excited as she dialed Sarah out in Brinnon, Washington. Lynn sat by, watching Penny make the call. Penny put the phone on speaker as they listened to the ominous sounding rings. Finally, the phone was answered by a loud barking.

"Damn it, Van Gogh, I told you not to pull on the phone every time it rings." There was a slight banging around of the phone before Sarah finally came on. "Hello?"

"Sarah? It's Penny Wickens from Las Vegas."

"Penny!" Sarah screamed into the phone. "I was going to call you this week to let you know Dave and I are coming down to visit."

"I know, and I also know you two are renewing your wedding vows."

"We are, how'd you find out?"

"Jim talked to Dave earlier about us coming up to visit you, but Dave told him about the wedding plans. I'm going to give you a fantastic wedding, leave it all to me. You just provide the bride and groom and I'll handle the rest. Do you remember Lynn from when we were kidnapped and brought here?"

"I do, is she in on your plan?"

"She's right here listening in."

"Hi, Sarah," Lynn piped up.

"Lynn, good to hear you again. Penny, will your plan involve bridesmaids?"

"You better believe it. I'll have a whole bunch of them for you. And we'll have a bachelorette party that will get us arrested."

"I don't think Dave would like that, but it's great to hear. Can I call my friend Connie out in New York to see if she can come?"

"You invite whoever you want, this is on me. I'll provide the plane travel and hotel stay. Just let me know who and how many. This will be so much fun."

"Thank you, Penny, I really appreciate you doing this for me."

"I'm doing this for me, too. I love weddings. Talk to Dave and see if he has any friends he wants to fly out, too. The more the merrier."

"How's Jim taking this?" Sarah asked.

"He's fine with you guys coming out, but I think he'll regret my plans. As long as we don't have an Elvis preacher, everything will go great."

"Now you got me all worked up. I won't sleep for days. I'll go talk to Dave and get this started on our end and call you back tomorrow."

"Great, I'll talk to you then." She said her goodbyes and hung up. She looked to Lynn, grinned, and said, "We need to call Shelby."

"This may cost you a fortune. Can you handle it?" Lynn asked.

"I've got plenty of money stashed away. Besides, if I run out, I can hit Jim up. He's got more money than I do, and he squirrels it away, so he'll have enough to cover it," Penny laughed.

~~*~~

Deacon read the name on the pad that Warren had filled out with the info about the missing husband. "We need to find out who this bookie Luther is."

Jim stood and said, "Follow me." He went out and down the hall to Trapper's office. Will Trapper was sitting at his desk on the phone.

"Sam, I got unwelcome visitors, I'll call you back later," he said into the phone.

"Wait," Jim yelled. "If that's Samantha, I need to ask her a question."

"Hold on, Sam, Jim needs to talk to you." He handed the phone to Jim as he came to the desk.

"Hey, Sam. How are you?" Jim told Trapper to put the phone on speaker.

"I'm good, Jim. What's up?" Samantha's voice came from the speaker.

"Deacon and I are following up on a missing husband who may have been involved with a bookie. Do you know one called Luther?"

"I do, he's bad news. If the man is involved with Luther and can't pay, Luther takes drastic actions. Not good for your man."

"Do you know where we can find him?"

"You really want to know? If Luther iced your man, it won't do much good to talk to him. It would be your neck. He doesn't like law enforcement."

"Well, we'll try not to look like cops," Jim said with a laugh. "I'd be very grateful if you'd give us the info."

"He has a store on Valley View that sells sex toys. Can't miss it, usually busy place. I'll get the address for you."

"Never mind, I know the place," Jim said coyly. "Not that I need to go in there, but I've been by the place."

"Take plenty of men with you, he has a bunch of goons that hang with him. Just be careful."

"Thanks Sam, I'll let you get back to Will." Jim nodded to Deacon and they left the room.

Jim and Deacon were walking down the hall to the back door when Penny and Lynn came flying out from the hallway. Penny was bouncing and came up to Jim.

"I talked to Sarah and we are getting it all arranged. This is going to be big. I can feel it."

"Don't overtax yourself. I don't want you wearing yourself out," Jim said.

"Lynn is going to help, and we called Shelby and she's getting some arrangements ready for Sarah to look at."

"How is she going to see these plans from all the way up in Washington State?"

"Jim, have you heard about this new invention called the internet? It will send pictures and text to anywhere in the world."

"Smart ass. Deacon and I have to go see a bookie, so stay out of trouble."

"A bookie, are you running out of money and now into gambling?"

"The last time I took a gamble was when I asked you to marry me. I learned my lesson."

Penny whacked Jim's arm and then gave him a kiss on the cheek. "That better be all the gambling you'll do. I may need your money for this wedding."

"We aren't marrying off the crown prince of England. Go easy on this."

"You really think I'll go easy, huh? Well, do you?"

"No, dear. I don't. Just have fun, you only live once. Now I have to go see a bookie." Jim kissed Penny and led Deacon out of the building.

They sat in Deacon's car. Deacon said, "You didn't mention to Penny that we were going to a sex shop."

"Are you crazy? She would have made a big deal out of it. But then again, she's getting so wrapped up in this wedding, she may have ignored it. Do you know where we're going?"

"Sure do. I've been in there, it's a startling place. I've never seen so many sex toys in my life."

"Why were you there?"

"Part of a murder investigation. We found a bag with the name of the store on it and went there to find out something about the person who bought the stuff. It is a strange place. I didn't see Luther, we weren't there to talk to him and didn't know it was a front for bookie operations. It's a good front."

"Well, I hope we don't have any problems." Jim thought for a moment and then said, "Hold on, I need to do something." Jim got out of the car and went back into the building, heading for Earl Daws' office. Earl wasn't in. Lacey came down the hall and told Jim that Earl was in the front. Jim went there and found him looking in a phone book.

"Looking for an escort service?" Jim asked.

"Yeah, and Paula would kill me. What's up, Sherlock?"

"Would you like to go defend me against a big, bad bookie?"

"Ah, a little action. Sure, right now?"

"Deacon's out in the car waiting."

"If you have Godzilla going with you, he must be a really big, bad bookie."

"I was warned by Samantha that he was dangerous. You know me, I'm getting too run down to handle thugs."

"Too old you mean. Let's go, I haven't bashed a head in a while."

They went out to the car and Deacon grinned seeing Earl was coming. "A little back up, Jim?"

"Yep, I'm not crazy. Now, let's go."

Deacon drove out and over to Valley View Highway. He pulled into the parking lot of the modest building and up to the front. They exited the car and went in. The shop was busy with men and a few women wandering around looking at all the sex toys and apparatuses of pleasure. Jim was amazed at the selection. Deacon went to the counter where there was a young woman in a bustier and short shorts.

"We need to talk to Luther," was all he said.

The girl stared at him, then looked Jim and Earl over. "Don't know any Luther."

Earl went to her and said, "Then you won't mind us looking in your back room."

"You have a warrant?" she shot back.

"We're not cops, so we don't need a warrant," Deacon said. "Now, is Luther in or do we start searching for him?"

Behind the girl a curtain parted and two very large black thugs came strolling out. "That's better, are either of you two muscle-bound-brainless-chumps named Luther?" Earl asked.

That pissed off one of the men, and he came around the counter at Earl. Now, Earl had tons of former training in black ops for the CIA and FBI. He was not a man to mess with. Earl took one good knuckle chop at the man's throat and he stumbled back. Deacon pulled his weapon on the other man. The first man was coughing hard and moved away as another, better dressed black male came out. He signaled to the two thugs and they went in the back.

"I'm Luther, what do you want?"

*

Chapter 5

He was tall, muscular and had a shaved head. He looked like a Luther. "I ain't got no time to talk to cops, so be quick, what do you want?"

Earl looked at Deacon and Jim, frowned and said, "We have to work on our image, do we really look like cops?" he looked back to Luther and said, "We're not cops, thank you. We're private investigators and we just want to ask a couple questions, that's all. Then you can go back to whatever you were doing. Not that I care, but my friends do."

Jim stepped forward and asked, "Do you know a man by the name of Bob Lenski? His wife said he talked to you last week."

Luther just stared, then slowly said, "Yeah, I know of him. Why you want to know?"

"It seems he's missing and his wife is concerned about his wellbeing. Have you seen or talked to him in the last couple days?"

"The man owes me some money, you really think he be crazy enough to talk to me? I ain't seen him."

"So you think he's hiding out from you? His wife said she had a visit from two big men the other day, could they be your men?"

"Don't know. I have many men who seek out people who owe me money. It could be they visited on the wife. I got no answer for you."

"Let's just say, hypothetically, that if your men found Bob, would they harm him?"

"If I need him to pay what he owes, it wouldn't do good to harm the man, now would it?"

Jim looked at Deacon, shrugged and said, "I guess that would be a good reason to not harm him. But your men could put a scare into him, maybe twist a finger or two?"

"My men have their ways of convincing a man to fulfill his obligation to repay his debts. Not that I condone it, but I let my men decide on how to be convincing."

"How much was he into you for?"

Luther started to look annoyed. "If you are trying to get me to admit to any wrong doings, I'd ask you to leave the store now."

Jim smiled, looked to Deacon, then Earl. "I guess Luther can't help us." He turned to the big man and said, "Sorry to interrupt your busy operation. Let's see, illegal book operation as I understand. The police and the casino owners would be happy to hear about this. All we need to know is where is Bob Lenski? Simple question, then we'll leave you alone."

Luther was trying to compose himself and took a big breath. "Look, I don't know where he is. You can try that loan shark he used to go to for cash to satisfy his bets. Stupid thing to do, bet one man's money against another."

"What's the shark's name?" Deacon asked.

"Whitley Harker. He be hanging around the casinos watching for big losers to snag for a loan to bet again. That's all I got to say. So, please excuse me." He turned and went back through the curtain.

"I know Harker, he's a sleazy little weasel," Deacon said. "We've picked him up before on suspicion of murdering men who owed him money."

"I keep saying, it doesn't make sense to whack someone who owes you money. They can't pay if they are dead," Jim said.

"Better to threaten a man with murdering his family if he doesn't pay," Earl said.

"Maybe Warren should keep an eye on Mrs. Lenski. Do you know where we can find Harker?" Jim asked Deacon.

"I have an idea where we can start. There's a small diner he hangs at. I'll take us there."

They went out to Deacon's car and drove to a dive called the Sunset Grill and parked. They went in and over to a booth. Deacon looked around, "I don't see Harker. He's not here."

The waitress came up and asked for their orders. Deacon spoke first, "Can you tell me if Whitley Harker has been here?"

"That scum bag? Yeah, he was here early this morning. Some guy showed up and they got into an argument over money. Harker left, followed by the man shortly after. Now, you want something to eat or just bust my chops?"

They gave her their orders for a light lunch and she went off. "I'll call Warren and see if Mrs. Lenski heard her husband mention Harker." He took out his cell phone and dialed. After a couple moments, "Greg, this is Deacon. I have a question." He paused for Warren to speak, then put his phone on speaker.

"Whatcha need?" Warren replied.

"Do you remember Whitley Harker, the loan shark we busted a couple years back?"

"Yeah, I remember him. Why?"

"Have you heard Mrs. Lenski mention his name?"

"No, but I know where Harker is." Warren said and then, "He's on ice in the morgue. They found him this morning, behind Harrah's Casino."

"How was he killed?" Deacon asked.

"Gunshot wound to his head. Looked like a perfect hit by a pro. Why?"

"Your missing man Lenski was in debt to him. I wonder if he did him in?"

"Well, that would be a twist. Hey, Boering is prowling around, so I have to cut this short. Talk later." Warren hung up.

"Interesting. Harker turns up dead and Lenski was in debt to him, too. Harker never used men to do his dirty work, so he had to be alone to be murdered," Deacon said.

The waitress came back with their drinks and Jim asked, "Can you tell us if Harker mentioned the name of the person he was arguing with?"

She paused, thinking. "I think I remember him calling the man Lensly, or Lensso, or something like that."

"Lenski?" Deacon asked.

"Yeah, that sounds like it. I'll have your food here shortly," she said and went off.

"I'm seeing Lenski murdering Harker," Jim said.

"Would be a reason for his disappearance. I doubt Harker carried any huge amounts of money on his body. If he did then Lenski may have taken it, then he could pay back Luther," Earl spoke after taking a sip of his drink.

"Since they found Harker this morning, and if Lenski got any money off him, I'd say Lenski would be going to see Luther today to pay him back. I'll call Greg and let him know," Deacon said. He pulled his cell phone and dialed Warren again. When he came on, Deacon quickly explained the situation. "We'll go back to Luther's and see what happens. Can you get away from the squad room?" He listened and said, "We'll see you there."

Their lunch came and they asked for doggie bags. The waitress gave them a dirty look and went back. "We better give her a good tip," Earl laughed.

She came back with the Styrofoam containers. Jim handed her a fifty and said, "That's for the food, the rest is yours." That made her smile, and she thanked them.

They went to the car and Deacon drove back to the sex shop. "We don't know what Lenski looks like. Can you ask Warren if he has a photo?" Jim asked.

Deacon pointed to Warren sitting in his unmarked car off the side of the parking lot. "Too late, he's here." They exited the car and went to Warren. He rolled down his window. "You got here awful fast," Deacon said.

"I was in the neighborhood. Shall we go in or just wait out here?" Warren asked.

"Do you know what Lenski looks like?" Jim asked.

Warren handed out a photo of the man. "I got this from the wife before she left the station."

The men looked the photo over and Deacon handed it back to Warren. "Nice looking guy. I hope he's not a murderer, too."

"I ran a check on him, he's clean, not even a ticket," Warren said.

"A man can snap under difficult situations, like owing money to a big, bad bookie. Maybe Lenski got desperate," Earl said.

They stood talking as a car pulled in and parked in front of the building. A man got out and looked around.

"Well, that's convenient and well timed. There's Lenski," Earl said. He went over followed by Deacon, Jim and now Warren.

Earl didn't say anything to spook the man, until he got right next to him, before he could enter the front door.

"Hey Bob, you have a minute?" Earl asked. Lenski looked startled.

"How do you know me?" he asked.

"We saw a photo of you that your wife gave me," Warren said, approaching the man and showing his badge.

A look of fear passed over Lenski's face. He turned to run but was surrounded by the four men.

"I didn't do anything," he said loudly.

"Did we accuse you of anything? We just want to know where you've been the last couple days. Your wife was worried," Warren said.

"I was…" he paused, thinking. "I was trying to find a person. I needed to borrow some money."

"Could that person be Whitley Harker?" Warren asked.

Now Lenski was really sweating bullets. "I didn't kill him," he blurted out.

"Did we say he was dead? How did you know?" Warren asked.

"I followed him from a diner and he went over to the back of Harrah's Casino to meet someone. I was hiding in some bushes watching, when this guy pulls a gun on Harker and shoots him. I waited until the shooter left and went to Harker. He was very dead. Okay, I did a bad thing, I took the money he had in his pocket. I had to. I had to pay Luther back. But I did make a call to the police about Harker being there."

Deacon said, "Do you have enough to pay Luther?"

"Just barely. But it's enough."

Deacon looked at Warren and said, "Let's let him pay his debt and then we can straighten out this mess."

*

Chapter 6

"Deacon, he stole money from a dead man," Warren protested.

"You know that. I know that, and so do Jim and Earl. Other than us, Lenski is the only other person who knows. If Lenski doesn't pay back Luther, his life and his wife's will be in danger. Harker isn't going to miss the money since he's dead, and if it isn't mentioned, no one will care."

"Boering will," Warren said, then paused. "Although, I'd like to have something that bastard doesn't know." Warren turned to Lenski and said, "Bob, you will go in and pay Luther, never mentioning where you got the money to him or anyone else. Understand?" Lenski nodded emphatically. "Then you will have to make a statement to the police that you witnessed the shooting. We'll work on your story about why you were there. You will never, ever mention that you took the money. Then you will get yourself into a program to stop your gambling. If you don't do this for yourself, do it for your wife."

Lenski looked on the verge of tears. Earl turned him around facing the door. "Go in and pay the man," he said. "I'll follow to be sure you don't get any grief." Earl opened the door for him and followed him in.

Jim said, "I think he needs more people," and he followed them in. Deacon and Warren brought up the rear.

At the counter, Earl said they needed to see Luther. The girl just stared. Earl leaned to her and growled, "Now!"

The curtain parted and out walked Luther. "Well, my favorite private eyes are back and you brought Lenski with you. Does he have my money?"

Earl poked Lenski and the man pulled a wad of money from his pocket and put it on the counter. "It's all there," Lenski said. "I counted it twice."

"Now, where might you have gotten all this money?" Luther asked.

Deacon stepped forward and said, "We took a collection at the precinct. My police friend here was very helpful in collecting."

42

Warren held up his badge and said, "Just take the money before I have this place raided. And don't ever take any more bets from Mr. Lenski again, understood?"

Luther gave them a big toothy grin and picked up the money. "It was nice knowing you gentlemen. Please leave before you scare away my customers." Then he turned and went back behind the curtain.

"I wonder if vice knows about this place?" Earl said as the men went out to the parking lot.

"Oh, I'm sure they do, but someone is getting paid to ignore the place," Warren said.

"Greg, are you saying that the police are corrupt?" Jim asked.

"I don't talk about that subject. I like my job, and shaking the boat is not a good thing to do," Warren said. He turned to Lenski, "I'm going to trust you to follow me to the precinct and make your statement about the hit on Harker."

Warren turned to the men and said, "Thanks guys, for helping. I'll let you know how it goes." He motioned to Lenski and they went to their cars.

"I love when a case comes together," Earl said. "Now, take me back so I can do my own work." He turned and went to Deacon's car.

"Are you or Lynn going to be taking the old woman's case about the stalker?" Jim asked Deacon as they went to the car.

"Lynn said she would, but then she got sucked into Penny's enthusiasm for the wedding. I'll see where her head is at, and I'll take the case if she's going to be too busy."

"Penny loves a good wedding. If Lynn is getting involved, she would be useless to you until Dave and Sarah are remarried," Jim said with a grin. "Let me know how the case is going. I'd like to know how my nasty reviewing nitpicker is doing."

They got in the car and drove back to the office.

~~*~~

"Penny, Lynn, it's so good to see you two again. Are you both still married?" Shelby Francis asked the women as they came into her wedding boutique. Shelby was the wedding planner for both Penny and Lynn's weddings.

"Of course we're both still married," Penny defended. "We're here to get another wedding started. I have a friend in Washington State who is coming into Vegas in less than two weeks to renew her vows. The first time they were here, they had a simple, quickie marriage and I'm not letting that happen again. You will outdo both mine and Lynn's wedding. Oh, and no Bridezilla murders this time," Penny said with a laugh.

"What kind of budget are we talking?" Shelby asked.

"Well, not the Prince William and Kate wedding, but not an Elvis presided one.

Somewhere in between. Shall we sit and work it out?"

The women gabbed and haggled over the details of what Penny expected. After almost two hours, they came to an agreement; it would be the Supreme Bride and Groom ceremony. One that Penny could afford, much to her delight. She loved Sarah and Dave, but didn't want to go broke for them. Although Penny wasn't poor, she had saved a small fortune over all the years she was on television. Between her and Jim they could live very well for the rest of their lives.

"If you could put together a package of details for this, I can email it to Sarah for her approval," Penny said.

"I'll get it ready and shoot it to you at your email address," Shelby said. "You do have an email address?"

"Of course, my personal email is pennylovesjim at gomail dot com. And, if you can include these photos, that would be great."

"I'll add all the wedding dress photos for Sarah to pick from, then she'll have to be fitted when she gets here. She's going to be a busy girl," Shelby said.

"That's all right. Now I want to be sure that the minister is not an Elvis clone," Penny insisted.

"No Elvis this time, I'll make sure. Well, that's all I need to start this, you just need to get the bride here."

"She'll be here. Thanks, Shelby. I'll watch for your email and send it to Sarah." Penny turned to Lynn, "Shall we go back and see what's going on?"

"Actually, I was supposed to follow up on the nasty woman reviewer, and talk to her stalker. I need to start that."

Penny and Lynn stood, thanking Shelby again, then they went out to Penny's car and drove back to the office. Lynn saw that Deacon's car was in the parking lot.

"I'm sure Deacon is going to bug me about the case. He agreed to let me follow up on it."

"He'll get over it, we had important things to do," Penny said as she parked. They went in and Penny went to Jim's office, while Lynn went to her own. Penny found Jim at his desk holding Willy.

"Look, Willy, Mommy has come back from conquering the wedding beast. And, she's not all bloody." Jim mocked to the dog.

"Very funny. I need your computer for a while," she said, going over to him and pushing him up.

Jim stood holding on to the dog. "What's up?"

"Shelby is emailing me details of the wedding and I have to send it to Sarah."

"Does Sarah have a say in her wedding?"

"Nope, I'm in charge. If she doesn't like it, she can go off and get remarried on her own."

"I love it when you take charge," Jim said, placing Willy on the desk as Penny turned on the computer.

"I have to call Sarah to see what her email address is. I'm surprised I never asked her before, we just seemed to always talk on the phone."

"Maybe she doesn't want to give her email address to you. You'd just end up sending her jokes and other spam."

"I don't send spam," she said as she pulled out her cell phone. "Now, keep quiet while we talk."

"I'll do better than that, I'm going out and visit Lacey." Penny was already dialing so Jim walked out of the room after picking up Willy. "Come on, puppy, we'll go find our own fun."

He went through the glass doors to the front lobby where he found Deacon and Lynn talking. Lacey was at her desk listening.

"So, how's the woman's case progressing?" Jim asked.

Lynn gave him a grin and said, "We're working on who will go after the stalker."

"Why don't you both go? Intimidation in numbers."

Lynn looked at Deacon, "I don't see a problem with that."

"It works for me. Do you know where he's at?"

"The woman left an address she got from sneaking a peek at the police report. I know the area," Lynn said.

"Okay, let's go start this before Mrs. Repas gets murdered," Deacon said with a grin. They said their goodbyes and left.

"Any good cases come in today, besides the nasty nitpicker," Jim asked Lacey as he put the dog down.

"Nope, it's been quiet today, for a change," she replied as Willy came bouncing over to her. She picked him up and set him on her desk.

"How are you and Mac getting along?" Jim asked about Lacey's husband and supervisor of Buck's security guards.

"All is good. We get along well, and with Jessie, we're a happy little family."

"Good. I hope it stays that way. Is Jessie doing well in school?"

"She is. Now if you don't have any more small talk to make, I have reports to file." She smiled and turned back to her desk.

Jim said he was going to see what everyone was up to and left the lobby. He went down the hall to Buck's office, but he was out. He went down to Trapper's, but he was out. "Nice, everyone has something to do," Jim mumbled to himself. He went to Earl's office, figuring he was still in, but he was gone too.

"Damn, I may as well go home and take a nap," Jim said, then jumped when he heard a voice behind him. It was Fred, the building's handyman and night watchman.

*

48

Chapter 7

"Feeling a little abandoned, Jim?" Fred asked.

"I'm glad everyone has something to do. Or, are they are out goofing off? I should check on things more often. This is my business and I should be more in charge."

"From what I've seen, this is a well-oiled machine. Everyone does what needs to be done, and gets it done. I listen when they talk, and they seem to have their jobs under control."

"Thank you for that, Fred. I appreciate the input. Where's Henry?" Jim asked about Fred's dog.

"He's out getting fresh air in the dog run. Do you want me to go get Willy and let him run with Henry?"

"Actually, that's a good idea. Why don't you go do that?"

Fred ambled towards the front just as Penny came flying out of the office. "So, did you get everything settled?" Jim asked.

"Yep. Shelby sent the files and I sent them to Sarah. She is so excited about the wedding. I don't know if she can wait. They want to get married on their anniversary, so we have to wait until then. But, she did say they would probably be out next week. Early, so they can get in some sight-seeing."

"I suppose you will be their tour guide for that?"

"As Sarah Palin would say, you betcha," Penny mimicked the woman.

"Are you going to run for president, Ms. Wickens?"

"I just may, I couldn't do worse."

"I'm not discussing politics, or religion." Jim went to his office as Penny followed.

"Coward. You have to have an opinion."

"My opinion is that I don't care. So drop it, please," Jim said as he entered his office with Penny on his heels.

"Just wait until we get in bed tonight. You will have an opinion or I'll roll over and go to sleep."

"Then you won't need No-Doze, and I'll sleep well."

Penny made a tsking sound with her tongue and left the room.

"I'm surrounded by crazy people," Jim said to himself. He turned to his computer and opened the chapter he was last working on for his latest book. He stared at the screen, not knowing what to write.

"Damn. I'm running dry. This is a fact based book, so why can't I write about that?" He realized that his memory was not up to par and he couldn't remember details about the case. He had often worried about Alzheimer's setting in, so waited until memory or inspiration took over.

He sat trying to gather his thoughts when he felt someone at his door, it was Buck.

"Hey, Jimmy. What are you doing in here on such a nice day?" Buck asked.

"I'm trying to write."

"Take a break and I'll take you out for an adventure," the big man said.

"Adventure? What have you cooked up?"

"Come with me and see." Buck walked away from the door heading to the back. Jim got up and followed him outside where he found Buck standing next to a brand new, huge GMC pickup.

"Where did you get this?" Jim asked.

"It's a gift to me. For my anniversary of being out here for four years."

Jim did some quick math and realized they had been in Vegas for four years. It didn't seem that long, but it was a special day.

"I'll have to order a buffet from Angelo's to celebrate. Does anyone else know?"

"Haven't asked. It was Penny, you and me who came out here first. Earl and Trapper came shortly after that. You go order the food, and later, we'll take a ride up in the mountains. This baby is a 4X4 with positraction."

Jim smiled and went back in the building to call Angelo. It was short notice, but Angelo said he could handle it.

After the arrangements were made, Jim went around and gathered everyone. Trapper and Earl had come back to their offices and wondered what Jim had going. Lynn and Deacon were still out talking to the stalker, but they would be back soon.

Angelo arrived with the food and Jim announced the reason for the celebration. He pulled

Penny close and said, "It was four years ago this month that Penny, Buck and I moved out here from Michigan. Never looking back. The rest of you followed like good friends and we appreciate it. So, enjoy the food, and the drinks are on me."

They were celebrating when Lynn and Deacon came back.

"So, did you find the stalker?" Jim asked them.

"Yeah, he was murdered," Lynn said with a frown. "Mrs. Repas was there with a real smoking gun. We called Warren and told him what we found. They have Repas in custody."

"That's one way to take care of a stalker. I presume they're booking her for murder?"

Lynn was gathering food for a sandwich from the table they had set out. "Yes, they are, and she's not denying it. She says she feared for her life and it was the only way to stop the man from killing her."

"Self-defense and insanity plea. Good try. Too bad Alphonse Grisler isn't still practicing law. This is right up his alley," Jim said.

"I don't think she did it," Lynn said.

"You said she had the smoking gun, what more do you need?"

"She was confused as to where she was. She was shocked that the man was dead. She didn't remember even going to his place and she said it wasn't even her gun. She doesn't own a gun."

"Well, you have your work cut out for you," Jim said.

"Do you want us to keep on her about this?"

"She's a client. Despite the fact she bashed my book, she deserves justice if she didn't do it. You have a tough case."

"Okay, we'll stay on it." Lynn paused, taking a bite of her sandwich, "By the way, what's with the food?"

"Buck reminded me that we came out to Vegas four years ago this month. So we're celebrating."

"It's been that long?" Lynn asked.

"Deacon came out here before we did to stay. You two have been together for over four years," Jim said.

"It feels like twenty," Deacon said, and got an elbow in his ribs from Lynn. "Oww."

Jim looked out the door of the break room and saw Trapper in the hallway with Samantha, his girlfriend and owner of an illegal bookie operation. Jim excused himself from Lynn and Deacon then went out into the hall.

"Hey Jim, how are you?" she asked.

"I'm fine. Haven't seen you in a while. What's up?"

"I have a problem, and I don't want the police involved. I thought maybe Will could help."

"Let's go to my office to talk." Jim led the way and they all sat in his office. "So, what's up?"

"I have one of my girls in the hospital. She's in bad shape according to the doctor. They say it was lead poisoning, severe lead poisoning. No one knows how she got it, but her body is shutting down. If I report it to the police, they may ask about her work at my place. As you know, I don't need police around my operation. But, I can't let this go without someone finding out how it happened."

"The doctors don't know how she got the lead into her system? Was she doing something with lead?"

"They say it wasn't ingested. They think it came through her skin. Her name is Monica, and she never did anything with lead. No hobbies or crafts that I know of. But for this amount of lead to cause her to be in such shape, it has to be something someone gave her in a big dose."

Jim looked at Trapper. "Are you going to investigate?"

"Yep. I'll see what I can find out and we'll go from there," Trapper said. "Sounds like a deliberate attempt to kill the girl. But how it was administered is the problem. I'll get on it today and let you know."

"Go to it, but if it's something more, then we'll have to let the police in on it."

"I'll use my discretion." Trapper stood, helping Sam up. "I'll keep you apprised of the situation."

They went out as Jim stayed at his desk. He was thinking about ways to kill a person with lead, besides a bullet. He turned to his computer, brought up Google, and typed in 'lead poisoning.' There were a whole lot of lead related subjects, and more than a few about the toxic poisoning aspect of it.

He read through a number of subjects when he heard someone enter the room. It was Penny.

"Why are you on your computer? We have celebrating to do," she said.

Jim looked at the computer and sighed. "You're right. Trapper can handle the situation." He stood and turned Penny towards the door. They went out and back to the lounge.

Angelo was picking up the empty trays and grinning as Jim came up. "Angelo, I need a bill for this food, no arguing. You've given us more than enough free food in the past."

Angelo smiled and took a folded piece of paper from his vest pocket and handed it to Jim. "Good, I'll have Lacey cut you a check. Now, I have a question. Do you know any ways of killing a person with lead?"

"Bullets. About the only way I know. But, one time there was a guy who would spray a substance on his enemies to kill them. I heard it was some high concentrate of that lead they used to put in gasoline."

"Thanks, I'll look that substance up. It may help."

*

Chapter 8

Tetraethyl lead was the name of the solution that could kill a person according to Google. One full strength cup on a person's skin would do the trick to kill. It was originally studied years ago by the U.S. War Department as a poison gas. It was fat soluble, so absorbed into the skin well enough. After studies, it was abandoned for the war effort to end up as an additive in gasoline to be an anti-knock solution in engines. After much uproar about the health effects of the additive, it was banned from use in gasoline. Now all gasoline is marked unleaded.

So, how did Tetraethyl lead show up to harm Sam's friend and employee. Jim called Trapper to see what was going on at the hospital.

"Jim, the woman passed away about a half hour ago. Sam isn't very happy," Trapper said on the phone.

"Did they find out what killed her?"

"Other than lead poisoning, no. They said it was enough to do her in. They just don't know how it was administered."

"Mention to them about Tetraethyl lead. It's a solution that will kill if put on the skin. It sounds like what may have happened," Jim said.

"That was a name they had mentioned, they're doing a tox to be sure, but they wanted to know how the solution was put on her body to be absorbed. Sam said she was a sun worshiper, and would slather her body with sunblock. I'm thinking it's a way that the lead got on her. Sam and I are going to her place to see what we can find."

"Good, keep me informed as to what you come up with," Jim requested.

"I'll do that, talk later," Trapper said and hung up. Jim sat back in his desk chair as Penny came in the room.

"So, what's happening with Trapper and Sam?" she asked.

"Oh, so you do listen to me when I talk," Jim said.

"Of course, sometimes you make sense. Not all the time, but occasionally. So what's up with the woman?"

"She died a half hour ago. Poisoned by lead through the skin, they say."

"I'm sorry for Sam. I know she cares for the women who work for her. Lead poisoning? How could that happen?"

"That's what Trapper and Sam are going to find out. They're going to the woman's apartment to see what they can find. From what they told me, I'm thinking it was from the sunscreen goop she put on her body."

"You're thinking lead could have been mixed in with the sunblock?"

"That's what I'm thinking, but we won't know until they find the sunblock. Has Angelo left?"

"Yep, he and his crew left and they did such a great job. I hope he does well with his catering."

"I'm sure he will. It's late, shall we go home?" Jim stood and went around his desk to Penny. She smiled as he put his arms around her and pulled her to him.

"If you're thinking of fooling around, at least lock the door," she said with a big smile.

"Fooling around? We don't fool around. We are serious in what we do. Also, you are forbidden to use sunblock when you are out at our pool, understand?"

"Whatever you say, boss. Shall we go home and continue this fooling around?"

"You find Willy and we'll be out the door. I have to check with Lacey first."

They broke their hold and Jim went to the front followed by Penny. Willy was on Lacey's desk, sleeping.

"That dog sleeps better than I do," Jim said. Penny went to pick him up as he raised his head when Jim spoke.

"You take cat naps, sleeping most of the day," Lacey said. "That's different than dog naps."

"Granted. Penny and I are leaving for the day. Since it's been quiet and we finished celebrating, you may as well close up and go home. I'll let anyone else in the building know you're leaving. Take Tracey with you. She is still working with us, right? I never see her out there. Did she get any of Angelo's food?"

"She did and she likes the quiet of the outer lobby. I'll let her know."

"Good, see you tomorrow," Jim said and led Penny to the back of the building. Jim checked the offices to see if anyone was in. The building was empty, so they went out the back door where they found Fred tending his flowers.

Penny went to her car and Jim stopped to talk to Fred. "How are you doing, Fred? Everything okay with you?"

"Everything is great and I'm totally happy to be working here. This beats living in the flood tunnels. Thank you for having me help out here."

"I'm glad you're here. The flower gardens look great. I'm heading home, don't get in trouble."

Fred laughed and said he wouldn't. Jim went to his Crown Vic and drove out.

~~*~~

Trapper followed Sam's directions to the apartments where Monica lived. "Did she have a roommate?" Trapper asked as he parked in front of the large building.

"I don't think she did. She never mentioned it otherwise. How are we going to get in?"

Trapper looked at her and said, "How long have we been going together? You should know by now that I have criminal talents. We'll get in." He opened his door and got out. Sam exited the car and followed him to the building. "Which apartment is hers?"

"Twenty-three upper." She pointed to the stairs going up and they climbed to the second floor. They went down the walkway and found the apartment. Trapper stopped and knocked.

"She lived alone, why are you knocking?" Sam asked.

"I just don't need any surprises. She may have moved a man in and if we go breaking in, he might get a little upset. It's better to check." He knocked again and got no response. "Okay, now we break in."

He pulled a small pouch from his coat pocket and took out a couple of thin tools. He worked on the door lock and had it open in no time. He pushed the door inward and waited. "No one is yelling, so I guess it's all right."

"What are we looking for?" Sam asked.

"Some jar or tube of any kind of body lotion. You said she loved to sunbathe, so look for sunblock. Don't get any on you, show me before you open anything."

Trapper went to a hallway and found the bathroom, Sam went to the kitchen. He nosed around all the beauty creams and paraphernalia on the counter, checking each bottle with a sniff. He figured the lead smell in the container would be masked by some perfume like lotion. But he knew what lead smelled like.

Sam came in and said, "I found this on the snack bar. Its sunblock that I've never heard of, and the label says it was made here in Vegas."

Trapper took the jar and opened it, taking a whiff. He thought it had a slight metallic odor that could be lead. He read the ingredients and said, "I'm sure if someone laced this with lead, they wouldn't put it in the ingredients. I'll have a friend of mine in LVPD have this tested." He put the cap back on and pulled a plastic bag from his pocket, putting the jar in. He looked around the bathroom again. "I haven't seen anything else that she would have put on her body in any amount that would do the damage. I think we have the evidence. Let's get out of here before we get caught."

They left the apartment and went back to the car. It was getting late, so Trapper said, "I'll have this checked in the morning. I'm sure LVPD forensics has gone home for the day."

"I thought CSI works 24 hours," Sam stated.

"They do, but the lab doesn't. Unless they changed the schedule, they didn't when I was on the force here. Of course, we didn't have as much crime. The mob ran the city and they dealt with problems in their own way. I'll drop you off and see you in the morning."

"Aren't you going to let me visit with you tonight?" she asked coyly.

"I thought we were cooling off a bit?"

"I'm cool enough, I wouldn't mind some company tonight. This whole thing with Monica has me a little upset."

"Of course, I'm sorry. You can come over and we'll relax."

"I hope you have plenty of wine. I need a bracer."

"I'll hit the store before we go to my place, just to be sure."

They drove out of the parking lot, unaware they were being watched from another apartment window.

"When do you figure you'll arrive?" Penny asked Sarah over the speaker phone at the snack bar.

"Dave said we are going to start driving early the day after tomorrow to beat the traffic. He figures the following day with one stop to sleep."

"So, three days from now you should be here?" Penny replied.

"It will be so good to see you and Jim again. How's Willy?"

"He's fine. I'm sure he and Van Gogh will have plenty to do."

"Dave and I debated on whether to take a plane or drive. With Van Gogh, we had to drive. Besides, it's easier to get around when we have a car. I looked over the email you sent with the gowns and I liked number three."

"Hold on while I take a look," Penny said as she opened the photos on her laptop. She scanned and found number three. "I love that one. You have good taste. Give me your sizes and measurements and I'll see if Shelby can get it ready for your final fitting."

"I'll email you the details, you can print them off and give them to her."

Jim stood in the hallway listening to the women talking. He turned and went back to his home office, he didn't want to get involved with the wedding plans. Penny would just bug him.

*

Chapter 9

"Here's the situation. Repas had gunshot residue on the hand that she fired the gun from. The bullets they removed from the author, Thomas Morton, matched her gun and the only prints on the gun were hers. How much more do you want?" Williams asked Lynn and Deacon.

"That proves she did it? I wouldn't be so quick to assume she did it."

"Lynn, she confessed. In interrogation, she said she got the gun from a neighbor and knew where Morton lived. We questioned the neighbor and he said that he loaned her the gun because she was afraid for her life at home. He didn't think she would take the gun with her to go kill the man. It's an open and shut case. Boering doesn't want us to waste time on this."

"Screw Boering, we want justice for this woman," Lynn said.

"You're going to make this a challenge, aren't you?" Deacon asked her.

"Damn right I am. I talked to this woman earlier. She doesn't seem to be the type to just up and kill a man."

"I thought she was a mean-spirited woman, and I think she was perfectly capable of doing this. If we hadn't arrived when we did and found her with the gun, she'd probably would have gone back home to write more bad reviews," Deacon replied. "She started with her crazy-in-the-head excuses as soon as we came through the door. How can you say she didn't do it? His body was still warm on the floor, and she was caught with the gun."

Lynn didn't say anything. She thought on it and looked at Williams. "She's not denying that she shot him?"

"She was laughing when she confessed. She enjoyed killing him. I'm sorry, Lynn, I know you'd like to follow up on this, but it is cut and dried. No one here that I talked to about this can see any other answer."

Lynn sighed, "I guess I wanted this to be a big deal. I was trying to like the woman, but she was mean. Okay, thanks, Williams." Lynn turned to leave as Deacon gave Williams a smile and followed her out.

"Not all cases are so easy. If we hadn't caught her, we'd be investigating the murder," Deacon said. "Are you okay?"

Lynn stopped at the door of her car and turned. "I was hoping that we would be able to solve this, but I have to admit that even we can't solve every case. Some are more useless than others. Let's go back to the office and see if we can find a real mystery to solve."

"I love it when you talk like a P.I. in heat," Deacon said with a grin. "But first, let's go home, it's late and I'm sure Jim has closed up the office.

~~*~~

Early the next morning, Jim crawled out of bed and chased Willy into the hallway. He went into his private bathroom, glad that he didn't have to keep it picked up for Penny. She kept her bathroom spotless; Jim wasn't a neat freak like her. It was fine with him as he was the only one to use his bathroom.

Thirty minutes later, he went out to the kitchen to start his toast. Penny was finishing her oatmeal and said, "I'll be stopping by today. Do you have any hot cases to work on?"

"None that I know of. Trapper is still tracking down the lead poisoning murder. Lynn and Deacon are trying to get my nasty nitpicker off of murder charges. Otherwise, it's been quiet."

"I hope it's going to be quiet when Sarah and Dave arrive tomorrow. If there's any big murder or terrorist cases, you're on your own. I called her and they are on the way. Sarah said Dave wasn't much for driving long distances, so she may do most of the driving."

"Smart man. I should have thought that when we drove up to their place."

"Oh, no. You don't like it when I drive. You get nervous, I've watched you," Penny replied.

"Yeah, when you drive like A.J. Foyt, I do get nervous. I'm surprised you don't have more tickets."

"I'm careful to watch for police. Now I have to go to work," she said and picked up her things, heading for the door.

"Be careful," Jim said quietly.

An hour later, Jim entered the office building to find Trapper and Sam in the back hallway. They turned to him and Trapper said, "Jim, I got the results from the sunblock I took to forensics this morning. It was a simple test and they said the jar was almost 80% tetraethyl lead. That much spread over a body would kill a person fairly quickly.

Smart of these deviants to put it in sunblock knowing the victim would cover large areas of his or her body."

"Anything on where the product came from?" Jim asked.

"The jar said it was made in Vegas. Otherwise, there was just enough on the jar to make it look like a legitimate product. Nothing as to where exactly it was made or what was in it. The label did say it was made in Vegas, but nothing to say where the company is. I'm going to see where the jar may have been bought. There's thousands of stores that carry products like this, I'm not happy about searching all of them."

"There was no price tag on the jar?"

"Nope, the thing could have been sold through a franchise run by people out of their homes. I'd say that is probably the best way. There was no UPC code on the jar, which is required to sell through a store. So it must be a private sale."

"Was there a product name on the jar?" Jim asked.

"Fun in the Sun. It was the only name that was on the thing."

"Did you look it up on Google?"

"Is everything solvable to you on Google?" Trapper said with a laugh.

"It sure helps. Let me know what you find out," Jim said and went to his office after saying hello to Sam.

Jim pushed the intercom button to connect with Lacey and said he was in.

Lacey's voice came back through the intercom, "I'll alert the press and send out a press release."

"You can be replaced," Jim said with a smile.

"Go ahead and try," she replied.

"Any new cases come in?"

"Nope, none you could handle."

"So, does that mean there were some cases coming in?"

"Two cheating spouse cases. But you don't like those." Lacey laughed through the intercom.

"Give them to Earl, he hasn't done much this week." Jim heard Lacey cut off the intercom. He sat at his desk and wondered what he was going to do now.

A few seconds later, Earl walked in. "I haven't done much this week? I helped you with the gambling man, didn't I?"

Jim smiled and said, "Yes, you did. I didn't know you were in the lobby to hear me."

"I took both the cheating spouse cases. Easy pickings to follow a spouse. What are you going to do?"

"I have guests coming in tomorrow and I don't want to be involved in murder or anything else that would disturb their visit."

"Talking about Dave and Sarah's wedding?"

"How'd you know?"

"I was part of that attack on Vegas by you, Dave and his FBI friend to find Penny and Sarah when they were kidnapped by the drug cartel. Besides, Penny told me."

"Yes, I forgot you did so well in helping take down the bad guys."

"I love it when you talk technical about crime. Bad guys. That's technical or generic?"

"Go chase your spouses. I need to organize my day."

"I better not find you napping today," Earl said as he left the office.

"Crazy people. I have crazy people around me." Jim said as he started his computer.

He typed in 'Vegas sunblock' on the Google page and it came up with nothing earth shattering. He did see one mention from a comment about a sunblock made in Vegas that made the person sick. He clicked on the link.

"I bought this sunblock from a woman selling it door to door and tried it on my arms. I got sick, and at the hospital they said I had some metal poisoning. They didn't seem very interested in helping me. They just told me to stop using the sunblock. I threw out the rest of the jar. Warning, don't buy anything from Meadow Springs distributors. Their product sucks."

Jim laughed at the nasty review for the sunblock, but it sounded like what Trapper was after. He stood and went to Trapper's office. He and Sam were at the computer reading.

"I suppose you saw the review about Meadow Springs products?" Jim asked.

"Yeah, we were trying to look up the company's address, but they seem to not have a listing. I'm thinking it's some person working out of their home, trying to poison people."

"The review I read said it was a woman who sold the product to the almost victim. I wonder if the woman was the person who poisoned the sunblock or if she was an accomplice?"

"Hard to tell. There was only one comment about the sunblock online. I guess there haven't been any other cases of poisonings," Trapper said.

Trapper's cell phone buzzed. He answered and listened for a few minutes then hung up. "Well, this is getting interesting. That was Larry in LVPD forensics. I went to see him this morning about the cream. He said that there have been two other cases of lead poisoning reported this morning. It's now a police matter."

*

Chapter 10

"Did those two other cases result in death?" Jim asked.

"One did, and the other victim is in bad shape. They don't think they can help her. Larry did talk to Warren when he came in to ask about lead poisoning, and Larry mentioned the jar of sunblock. I have a feeling that Warren may visit us to take our jar," Trapper said.

"You still have the jar?"

Trapper reached into his desk drawer and took out the jar, still in the plastic bag. "Larry did a quick dusting for prints, he'll get back to me on that later. He scooped out some of the lotion for testing and I took the jar back."

Trapper reached across the desk, handing the jar to Jim. Jim examined the jar through the bag, turning it around to read the label. "It was printed on an ink-jet printer. Some of the label is running from getting wet. As you said, no address or info about the company other than the name, and that it's for protection from the sun." Jim looked at Sam and asked, "Did Monica ever say anything about buying beauty products from some home distributor?"

"She never mentioned it to me. I'll ask the other women if they heard her talk about it," she replied.

Trapper said, "Give them a call and ask. Before Greg Warren comes in and claims the case."

Sam pulled out her cell phone, excused herself, and went to the hallway. Jim moved to Trapper's desk. "So, what do you think?" Jim asked.

"Murder. And it may not be the end. With these two other cases of poisoning, it could be just the beginning. Remember the Tylenol scare years ago? Someone was poisoning Tylenol and it caused a huge ruckus around the world."

"Lots of people use Tylenol, not everyone uses sunblock. I know it's Vegas, and the sun can cause problems for people working or playing outside for extended periods of time. So, sunblock is big business here. If someone is spiking sunblock with Tetraethyl lead, it's murder."

"We just need to know where this jar came from. I hope Sam can find one of her girls who had talked to Monica about where she got this sunblock."

They heard voices from the hallway and turned to see Greg Warren enter with Sam. "Look who I found wandering the hallway," Sam said.

"Greg, what brings you here?" Trapper asked. "I imagine I already know. May as well sit while we explain our story."

"Thanks, Will. Do you have the jar of sunblock that Larry told me about?"

Trapper looked at Jim, who still held the jar. "It's been dusted and tested, but you should already know that," Jim said. He reached out and gave Warren the jar.

"Boering assigned me to follow up on this. I think he wasn't happy that I kept following the missing husband, Bob Lenski. I made up a story for Bob to tell about how he was involved in the hit of Harker. I don't think Boering believed it, but couldn't prove anything anyway. So talk to me about the lead poisoning."

Jim motioned to Sam to sit in a chair next to Trapper's desk and then he sat next to Warren.

"So, what do you know, Greg?" Jim asked.

"We had two women collapse at the pool behind the MGM Grand. They were both friends from what their companions told us. I had to go back and get the sunblock that they left at the pool. Larry said it had some fancy-named lead in it that would kill people if it was spread on their skin. Larry mentioned that you had the same problem."

"What was the product you got from the pool. Was it like that jar?" Trapper asked pointing to the jar Warren now held.

He looked at the jar, read the label and said, "No, we got tubes of sunblock filled with lead. They had the same labels on them, Fun in the Sun Lotion, but not in jars."

Jim looked to Trapper. "They're adding to their product line. Are you going to warn the public?" he asked Warren.

"I suggested it to Boering, but he said it would just cause a panic. The manufacturers of good sunblock may not like having their products smeared." Warren laughed at his double meaning. "I think if someone outside of the police warned the media, it might help." Warren gave Jim and Trapper a sly grin.

"Gee, I know one person on TV who would be more than happy to warn the public. Maybe someone on the TV news might like to spread this also, it could go viral," Jim said.

"Whatever you do, I don't know anything about it. You are on an investigation of your own and feel that the public should be aware of this possible threat. That's all Boering has to know," Warren said.

"Don't worry, we won't blow your cover. Now, how long did it take for the lotion to take effect on the women by the pool?" Trapper asked.

"From what the friends said, they applied the lotion, and within a half hour they were getting sick. One girl only put it on her arms and face. The other girl, the one who died, covered most of her exposed skin. I can't find the distributor of the product and none of the friends knew where they got the sunblock from."

"I think I may have an answer," Sam said. "I called my office and talked to my head girl. She said that Monica mentioned she got beauty creams from some woman who lived in her apartment building. No word as to who, but the woman lived there."

"Well, it's someplace to start," Jim said. "Greg, care to join us and make it a police action?"

"I'm fine with that. As long as Boering leaves me alone. Shall we go?"

"I'll let Lacey know we're going out, and then meet you out back," Jim said, stood, and went up front.

The rest of them stood and went out the back door, waiting for Jim by the cars.

"I gave Penny a quick rundown on what she needs to say on her show about the sunblock," Jim said, as he came out. "Now where did Monica live?"

"I've already been there, so follow me," Trapper responded. "Greg, can you keep up?"

"Don't worry about me, I'll follow you."

Jim went with Trapper and Sam as Warren followed in the unmarked cop car.

Ten minutes later, they parked in the lot of the apartment building. They stood looking at the two large two-story buildings.

"There's a lot of apartments there. I hope the first couple ones we ask know where this Fun in the Sun seller is," Trapper said.

"Well, let's get to it," Jim said. "I'll go with Warren to that building, and you two go to the other."

They split up. Warren and Jim went to the first door on the bottom floor. They knocked and the door opened. An older woman glared at them through the partially opened door. "If you are selling anything, I'm calling the police," she growled.

Warren smiled and held out his badge, "I am the police, ma'am. We just need to ask one question, then we'll leave you. Do you know anyone in these apartments selling beauty products called Fun in the Sun?"

She did some thinking, or they thought she was thinking. She smiled and said, "No, I don't. Goodbye." She slammed the door.

"We must have caught her watching her soaps," Jim laughed. They went to the next apartment and did the same thing. After clearing the first floor with rejections, they climbed the stairs and proceeded to start at the first door at the top of the stairs. A woman answered and they asked her about any products being sold. The woman looked upset when Warren identified himself as a cop.

"I'm sorry, I don't know about any sales of sunblock here in the complex," she said nervously.

"We didn't say anything about sunblock," Jim said. "Why did you mention that?"

"Because she sells the sunblock," came a voice from the stairs as Trapper and Sam were coming up.

The woman panicked and tried to slam the door, but Warren put his shoulder into it and pushed it back. Just inside the door they could see boxes on the floor. They were all marked with the word 'lotion' on the sides.

The woman ran to another door and went through it. Jim saw it was the bathroom before she closed the door. "She's not going too far. Unless she climbs out the window." Sam said she'd go watch and went back downstairs.

Warren went to a box on a stack of five and opened the top. He pulled out a jar that had the same label as the jar they had. "I think we found our source," he said.

"I don't see any equipment to load the lead into the jars, or any containers of lead. This must not be the place where they're making the product," Jim said.

They heard a screaming coming from the outside and went out the door. They could see Sam coming up the stairs with the woman in an arm lock. Warren went to them as they hit the top stair and he took her from Sam.

"She was hanging off the window in the back as I came around. She dropped right into my arms," Sam said.

Trapper looked at Jim and said, "She's one tough broad."

"You better believe it," Sam replied.

Warren pulled the woman to a chair and set her down. "Now, I think you really need to start talking. First, who are you?"

*

Chapter 11

The woman sat quietly. "Look, you better start talking. Your sunblock has been involved in two murders so far. You really need to talk now."

The woman still said nothing. Then she said, "I want my lawyer."

Warren looked frustrated, then pulled her up and turned her around. He grabbed her wrists and applied his cuffs on her. "Fine, you are under arrest for accessory to murder in two homicides. We have the evidence in your apartment, and you did attempt to flee. Resisting arrest is not good." He read her the Miranda and asked Trapper to find her keys to lock up the apartment until CSI could take over. Warren took the woman out of the building as they looked for keys. Sam found them on a counter in the kitchen. They locked the door and went back down to the cars.

Warren had the woman in the back of the unmarked car and was making a phone call. Trapper handed him the keys and waited. Warren finished his call and said, "We found the source of the sales, but we need to find where this stuff is being made and packaged."

"I don't know," came a voice from the back seat of the car.

Everyone leaned down for a better look as Warren leaned in. "You're going to talk now?"

"I don't know where the stuff is being made. I answered an ad to sell the stuff for extra income. That's all. They delivered the boxes here and I was to sell them. They told me to keep half of the money and they'd come by to collect the rest once a week. That's all I know. "

"So why did you run?"

"I heard from another woman I sold the stuff to that she was getting sick. I opened a jar and it smelled strange. Then I heard about Monica through a mutual friend, that she died. I wasn't sure if my stuff did it. Then you showed up and I panicked."

"Do you know those jars are filled with lead? Enough to poison whoever uses the lotion."

"I don't know what's in the jars, just that it was good for sunblock. Vegas is a good market for sunblock, so I got involved. I've only been at it less than a week."

"How many other jars have you sold?" Warren continued to question the woman as long as she was talking.

"I sold one to Monica, and a couple to some women at my work. Only three."

"The one box I saw had jars. Do you sell any in tubes?"

"Tubes? No, just jars."

Warren stood up and said to the others, "There must be more people selling this crap. We need to get this out quickly, to warn people."

"I'll have Penny call her station to get it on the news," Jim said and went off the side to call.

Warren asked the woman, "What's your name?"

"Roxanne Lyons," she replied.

"Okay Roxanne, I don't think you intentionally tried to murder people, but that's for a jury to decide. Do you have any information as to where we can find your supplier?"

"I just have a phone number. They never told me where they were or who they were."

"Okay. After CSI gets finished with their inspection of your apartment, you'll be questioned again. So, if you cooperate, it may go easy for you."

She sat looking lost. Warren closed the car door and turned to the others. "I'm not believing she intentionally tried to kill people. We need to find the source now that we know how this stuff is getting out."

Jim came back and said, "I told Penny everything about the situation and she's calling her station. She said they should have it on the next news broadcast. Once her station picks it up, the others will follow, so Boering should be pestered about the sunblock."

"Great, he's going to blame me," Warren moaned.

"It's his damn job, Greg. If he doesn't like it, he'll have to deal with me. I never liked the man," Trapper said.

"We'll see. As soon as backup and CSI get here, we'll take her in. Maybe I can head off Boering before the crap hits."

A half hour later, they were bringing Lyons into the station. Boering was in the squad room staring at the parade of people coming in. "What's going on here, Warren?" he barked.

"We found this woman selling the poisoned sunblock. She's part of a group of home sales people pushing the lead laced sunblock. She has information as to where we may find the people making the product.

"Put her in interrogation," he said. Warren took the woman out of the room as Boering turned to Trapper. "What are you doing here, Trapper? Who pulled your string?"

"You haven't changed, Harvey. You're still an ass."

Boering went up to Trapper, trying to go nose to nose with him, but Boering was a few inches shorter than Trapper.

"I can have you ejected from here," he snarled.

"Will Trapper!" came a voice from across the squad room. It was Captain Weber. "What the hell are you doing here?"

Boering smiled, figuring Weber was going to give Trapper a hard time.

"I'm helping to investigate a murder, Captain," Trapper said, as Weber came over. He pushed Boering aside and gave Trapper a hug.

"You old weasel, good to see you. Now what's this about a murder?"

Trapper gave him the quick version of the case and that Warren had the woman in custody.

"Warren is a good cop. He'll get to the bottom of this." Weber suddenly saw Jim and Sam. "Jim, Sam, how the hell are you both?"

Sam went to Weber, "I'm fine, darlin', good to see you." Then she whispered as she hugged him, "You haven't been around to see me, are you no longer gambling?"

Weber cleared his throat, "We can talk about that later. Now, I want all the details about this sunblock case. Let's go to my office." He grabbed Trapper's arm and pulled him to the hallway to his office. He looked back and said, "Boering, don't just stand there, do something."

Trapper grinned while Boering looked shocked and flustered.

Weber, Trapper, Jim, and Sam all sat in Weber's office. Trapper gave the details of the case.

"My God, this is terrible. The news people should know about this," Weber said.

"I talked to Penny and she's sending off word to her station, it should hit all the channels by six."

"Good, this is not something Vegas needs. Is Warren going to interrogate the woman?"

"He took her to interrogation, I'm not sure if he's started," Trapper said.

"Well, let's go see," Weber said and stood. They all went out and over to the interrogation rooms. Warren was standing outside one room watching the woman. He stiffened when Weber approached.

"Good job finding this woman, Greg. Have you talked to her yet?"

"I was just making her sweat a little. I don't think she knows much. She just sold the product, but if I can find the people who are making this stuff, we'll stop them."

"Very good, you take charge and keep me informed." He turned and went off into the hallway.

"He hasn't changed much, hit and run," Jim said.

"Weber tries to do as little as possible," Warren said. "That's why he hated to lose Lynn and Deacon. They did so much for him."

"You'll fill that gap, Greg. Don't worry," Trapper said.

Warren turned to the glass and said, "I think she's had time to stew. You guys can relax in observation." He went to the door and in as the others went to the next door.

"I think Greg has come a long way from when he was second to Deacon," Jim said.

"He'll do fine if they can get rid of Boering," Trapper said.

In the room, Warren sat across from Lyons. "Roxanne, I don't think you were in on the scheme

83

to murder those women. But, it would be to your best advantage to help us find the people behind this." He waited for a reaction.

"Honestly, I was just trying to make an extra buck or two. I work at Sonic as a waitress. I'm on part time and the pay isn't the best. I saw an ad in the Review Journal about making money in my spare time selling sunblock. Hey, it's Vegas, it's always sunny. So it sounded easy. I called the number and they sent over a pickup truck with boxes of jars. I found out I'm not much of a sales person. I was afraid to approach people. I knew Monica through friends and I saw her the other day, so I brought up the sunblock. She loved to sit in the sun, so she bought a jar."

"Okay, do you have the phone number to the people?"

She pulled her cell phone out of her pocket and went through the contacts. "Yeah, it's here."

She handed the phone to Warren, he studied it and wrote the number on the pad of paper that was on the table. He tore off the top sheet and handed the pad to Lyons and said to write down everything she knew about how she got involved in the scheme. He took the phone and put it in a plastic evidence bag he had in his pocket. He excused himself and went out and over to observation.

"Not much to ask her, she's not really into the deep crime of the case. Later, I think I'll have her call this number and tell whoever that she needs more product. If we can nab them, we may have something.

*

Chapter 12

"I think you should call them before the news goes out to the public. It may scare them off," Jim said.

"Or make them change direction. What else could they put this lead in that would kill people?" Trapper asked.

"I can't think of much. But, I don't know who these people are or why they're doing this. I'm torn over how we should do this. Tell the news to hold off on warning people so we can set up a sting, or blow the situation by sending out a warning and watching the criminals back off," Warren said.

"I think the priority is to save lives. If these people back off, it will give you time to find them. Also, if other distributors hear about the products they are selling, they may come forward and warn people they sold this crap to," Jim said.

"True, we'll wait and see what the news effect has," Warren sighed.

"What about her?" Sam asked, looking at Lyons through the magic glass.

"We have the product, and she admitted to selling it to Monica. We have to treat her like a drug dealer who sold the product to people. I hate to do it to her."

"She admitted she had no idea that the sunblock was laced. She worked in good faith and she shouldn't be punished. Drug dealers know what they are selling is dangerous," Jim offered.

"I'll keep her overnight, until we see what the news broadcast does. I really want to cut her loose, but it may be better for her to wait it out," Warren said. "If other sellers come forward, it will look better for her."

"I think we need to coach the news as to what to say. Have them ask other dealers for cooperation to turn any products and sales lists they have over to the police," Jim said. "Let's go see Penny and talk to her. We still have a couple hours before the news hits. Besides, if you call the criminals now, they may not be able to deliver today. The news will come out and they will just retreat into the woodwork."

"Very true, and the first priority is to save lives. Let's go see Penny." Warren told a uniform to take Lyons to a holding cell for the night.

They went back out to the squad room and Boering gave them a dirty look, but didn't bother them. They went through the room and out the back to their cars.

Shortly after, they were back at Jim's building and found Penny with Lynn and Deacon in Lynn's office.

"I called Gordy and he's setting up a meeting to get the facts about the murders. They don't want to screw up with unsubstantiated facts. He said he'd call me when they are ready," Penny said.

"Well, with Warren with us, they'll have the facts from the police. That should be good enough," Jim said. "Do they want us at the station?"

"Gordy said it would be better. I was just about to call you when you came in."

"Then let's get a jump on this and go there," Warren said. Everyone was getting ready to go.

Jim looked to Lynn and asked, "Are you continuing to follow the annoying nitpicker's murder charge?"

"No, I did talk to her this afternoon and I'm really believing she killed the author. Besides. she told me we were off the case."

"So, we didn't get paid for the time you were on it?"

"Nope, she's not paying. She's one mean woman, hope she gets life."

"Come on, Jim," Penny yelled from the hallway. Jim grinned and left the room.

Jim and Penny went in Jim's car as Trapper followed with Sam. Warren brought up the rear. They arrived at the station and Penny called Gordy to say they were coming in. They entered the news room and Gordy waved them to come over.

"Penny, you know Howard Keller, News Director. He's very interested in hearing this story."

Penny said, "I don't know all the facts. Warren is with the police and can tell you more than I can." She stood aside and let Warren talk.

Warren held his hand out to Keller, they shook and Keller said, "Talk to me."

Everyone sat as Warren explained the case. He finished up by saying, "We need to stress the fact that there may be more of this sunblock out there with other distributors. They need to bring the cases of sunblock to the police. Plus, they should warn the people who did buy the product that there is a potential for death."

Keller asked, "Detective Warren, do you have any idea who the people are who are making this substance?"

"Not at the moment. Because we are warning people about the product, it will probably force them into going deep. They won't be able to manufacture sunblock. We hope they don't change directions. Our first job is to save lives, then catch these bastards."

There was a man sitting behind Keller writing on a pad. Keller pointed to him and said, "This is Bill Dowe, he's our head writer and he will take this. We'll get this out on our five o'clock news, then we'll release it to the other stations for their six o'clock update. I hope this will help to catch the bastards. Detective Warren, please get with Dowe and be sure the facts are all there. I'll leave it up to you, I have other duties I have to perform." He thanked them and left the room.

Warren went to the man and sat next to him. "What have you got so far?"

Dowe read the copy he created and everyone listened. He finished and looked to Warren. "I think that covers it," Warren said, and looked to the others. They all agreed and Dowe said he had to get it programmed on the teleprompter.

They had about 30 minutes before the news would start. Dowe had said it would be the breaking news report at the top. He pointed to a monitor in the corner and said they could watch. Penny picked up the remote and turned the TV on.

"Think this will help?" Sam asked.

"Depends on how many people will be watching the news," Jim said. "Hopefully, the newsprint media will pick up on it also. If I don't see anything in the Review Journal tomorrow, I'll make some calls. People still do read the paper."

Warren's cell phone buzzed. He answered, listened, then hung up. "That was Williams, it's getting worse, more people are getting sick, and there were two more deaths."

Everyone was silent until the news came on. "Good evening, we have a breaking news story that is very important for you to listen to," The anchor said. "There is a warning from Las Vegas Police that there is sunblock being sold through home distributors that is laced with deadly lead poisons. If you purchased any product from Fun in the Sun brand sunblock sold through Meadow Springs, do not use it. There have been four deaths associated with the cream. If you are a distributor, please bring all of your supply to your local police station. Any person harboring this product will be prosecuted. It is imperative that this product is not used. If you purchased the product, do not destroy it or throw it out, bring it to a police station and inform them as to who sold it to you. Again, do not use any sunblock labeled from the Fun in the Sun brand purchased from a Meadow Spring distributor. It contains Tetraethyl lead that will cause death."

The news cut to less important stories. Jim spoke first, "Well, that should be enough to start a panic. Greg, I think you need to go back to the precinct. It may get busy."

Warren stood, then said, "I'll let you guys know what is going on. I'm sure this will stop the people responsible for packaging up this stuff. I think we have a little breathing space now. Thanks guys, for helping and for giving Weber the idea that I was behind this." Warren turned and went out of the room.

"Maybe Greg will get a little respect from this," Trapper said.

"I hope so," Jim said. "I think our part in this is done for now, until Greg gets some intel about who may be making the stuff. Hopefully, they won't use some other method of delivery for the lead now that the sunblock method has been exposed."

"I can't think of any other way. They couldn't put it in the water supply. They would need a tremendous amount of the lead to work that way. Our water supply would just dilute the lead."

"Well, we'll find out in a few days if people start dropping." Jim turned to Penny and said, "Let's go rescue Willy and go home. I'm tired, and this has been a long day."

Penny stood and kissed Jim and agreed. "Trapper, I'll see you in the morning if nothing else breaks tonight. But, it's up to Warren to handle it now."

They went out and back to the office to get Willy. They pulled into the back parking lot and found Fred with Henry and Willy in the dog run. Willy started bouncing around when he saw them. Jim told Penny to get the dog, he was going to check with Lacey.

He went into the building and to the front. Lacey was at her desk talking on the phone. Jim stood waiting for her to finish.

She hung up and looked at Jim, "Well timed. That was Deacon, he couldn't get through to your cell phone, and he said Lynn is in LV Medical. She has skin poisoning from some facial cream she applied.

*

Chapter 13

Jim felt a chill. "Did he say it was sunblock?"

"No, some kind of moisturizing cream she put on her hands. She started feeling sick and was vomiting, so Deacon took her to LV Medical. He heard about the sunblock and didn't know it could be in the hand cream."

"Did he say how she was doing?"

"He got her to the hospital and they are doing the best to reverse the poisoning. That's all he said before he had to go."

"Thanks," Jim said and rushed out towards the back door. He found Penny talking to Fred and said, "Let go, quickly. Lynn is in the hospital with skin poisoning."

"What!" Penny yelled as she followed Jim to the car. She jumped in after leaving Willy with Fred and asked, "What happened?"

"I don't know. Lacey said Deacon called the office, he couldn't reach me on my phone."

"The TV station has so much electronic equipment running, it probably messed with your signal. So where is she?"

"Lacey said she's in LV Medical. I didn't ask what room, but I'm sure we'll find Deacon when we get there."

Jim drove as fast as he could without causing any traffic problems or attracting a cop. They arrived at the ER entrance and Jim parked in front. They entered the ER entrance and rushed to the desk.

"Do you have a Lynn DeAngelo admitted with skin poisoning?" Jim asked the nurse behind the counter.

"Honey, we got lots of skin poisoning patients in tonight. Take a number."

It's not what Jim wanted to hear. "Listen Nurse, Lynn DeAngelo is a cop and she's here somewhere. Look her up!" Jim lied a little, but he wanted to put a fire under the nurse.

She stared at Jim and then looked to Penny. "Hey, you're that talk show lady."

"Yeah, yeah, can you just tell us where Lynn DeAngelo is?" Penny said impatiently.

They heard a voice behind them, it was Deacon. "Jim, Penny, thanks for coming," he said.

"How is she?" Jim asked.

"They have her stabilized and got the cream off her skin. Luckily, I got her here in time before it soaked into her system. The doc said she will be all right."

"What happened?"

"She was complaining about her dry hands and pulled this tube of moisturizer from her purse and applied the cream. She started to complain that her hands were burning and then she started to get sick.

I grabbed her and rushed her here. She's resting now, they say."

"Do you have the tube of the cream?" Jim asked.

Deacon pulled a plastic bag from his pocket with the tube. He handed it to Jim. "It's different from the sunblock, from what I've heard about it."

"Where did she get this?"

"She doesn't remember. It's been in her purse for a couple weeks she said. I don't think she was able to think straight. I'll take the tube to Larry and have him examine it."

They looked to the entrance as Warren came in. "I called him," Jim said.

"Deacon, how is she?" Warren asked.

"She's stable now, Greg, thanks." Deacon went through the story again for the detective and showed him the tube.

"It's not the same as the sunblock," Jim said. "Different label name and manufacturer."

"Damn, they've already branched out with this crap," Warren said. "Now we have to warn people not to use any lotion on their skin."

"That's going to make a lot of women unhappy if they can't cleanse their skin and apply make-up," Penny said.

"And the alternative is dying?" Jim said. Penny didn't reply.

Warren said, "I'll get this back to forensics and see that they do a quick tox on it."

"Thanks, Greg," Deacon said.

"Tell Lynn I'm glad she's all right," Warren said, and left with the lotion tube.

"I hope the news break helped people realize there's something wrong with putting anything on their skin," Jim said.

"But, they only covered sunblock, this was moisturizer," Penny said.

Jim thought a moment then said, "Maybe this was an early test to see if the stuff works."

"Where do you think Lynn got the tube?" Penny asked.

"We'll have to ask her when she's able to talk," Deacon said. "All we can do is wait until the doc says she's awake. They have her medicated." Deacon motioned to the waiting room and they went in.

"Did you find out anything on the sunblock?" Deacon asked.

Jim covered everything that happened earlier in the day up to the news broadcast.

"I was watching the news when they announced it. That's why I figured Lynn had the poisoning. As soon as she started getting sick, I rushed her here," Deacon said.

"Where's the baby?" Penny asked.

"She's with the lady who lives next door, she's watched the baby before."

They made small talk for another hour, then a doctor came to talk to Deacon.

"Mr. DeAngelo, your wife is awake and she's doing very well. You can go see her now," he said.

The three of them went to the private room Deacon requested. Lynn was sitting up now and drinking through a straw, as a nurse was adjusting the intravenous tubes that ran to Lynn's arms. The nurse waved to them to come in.

"Hey baby, how are you feeling?" Deacon asked as he moved to the bed. She smiled and put the drinking cup down.

"Like I was run through a car wash. I'm still feeling dizzy, but starting to get out of it."

Jim moved forward. "I'm glad you're all right, but where did you get that hand cream?"

Lynn swallowed, "It came in the mail the other day, in a sample box. I wasn't aware of the sunblock problem then. I put the tube in my purse and forgot about it until today. My hands were so dry, they hurt. But, not as bad as after I put the crème on. Is it the same crap as the sunblock?"

"Don't know yet. Greg Warren took the tube in to have it checked. He should let us know anytime," Deacon assured her. "I'm glad I got you here quickly and you only put the stuff on your hands."

"So am I," Lynn said and looked to Penny. "Does this mean we can't use any lotions on our skin?"

"I certainly hope not. I still have plenty of lotions that I've been using, so I'm not worried about any older ones." Penny turned to Jim, "I should go call the station and let them know about this new development."

"Tell them to warn people not to use any products that aren't purchased from a store. Especially off brand types of products," Jim said.

"I'll be back. They don't like us using cell phone in the building." She left the room as Deacon leaned over to kiss Lynn.

"You must be tired. Why don't you get some rest and I'll go rescue Mrs. Wycof and get the baby. I'll come back after I see if Paula can watch her for a while."

Lynn agreed and used the remote to lower the bed. Deacon and Jim said their goodbyes and left the room.

"I'll call Warren to see if he has any results from the lotion," Jim said as the got to the lobby. "I'll call you when I hear something."

"Thanks, Jim. It was good of you and Penny to come down to see Lynn, I appreciate it."

"Hey, you two are our friends. We take care of friends."

Penny came back in and said, "I talked to the news department and they are going to cover the development on the next news broadcast."

"Good, let's go back and get Willy, then go home. It's been a long day."

Penny said goodbye to Deacon and they left. Jim drove back to the office and parked. Fred must have been inside, the dogs were gone, also. They entered and were attacked by both dogs. Jim reached down and picked up Willy as Fred came out of his room.

"So, how is Lynn?" Fred asked.

"Good so far, thanks for asking. I have to go warn Lacey and Tracey about the skin stuff," Penny said and went down the hall.

"Lacey said you two got a call from some woman coming in from Washington State."

"Wow, I forgot about them. Thanks, Fred. I'll go warn Penny." Jim went through the hall to the front where he found Penny, Lacey, and Tracey standing in front of the counter. Penny was explaining to them to avoid any unknown type lotions for a while. Jim stood waiting.

Penny turned to Jim and said, "Shall we go home?"

"Lacey told Fred that Sarah called."

Lacey took a breath and said, "Oh, yeah. I forgot. Sarah called and said they are stopping for the night and expect to arrive in Vegas before noon tomorrow. She said she tried to call your cell phone but just got voice mail."

Penny pulled out her cell phone from her purse and found it was shut off. She looked at Jim and said, "Now I'm doing what you always do. Shutting off the phone and not remembering it." She turned it back on and listened for the messages. When she was done, she put it back in her purse. "Sarah said what Lacey said. They're going to a motel for the night and will be here tomorrow.

Damn, I'm all turned around by all this commotion. I hope I can be ready for them."

"Well, dear, shall we go home so you can rest up?" Jim said. "I'll even let you get a good night's sleep."

She took Willy and went to the back. Jim turned to Lacey, "We probably won't be in tomorrow, so just take messages for me."

"That won't be hard, no one ever calls for you," Lacey replied.

"You can be replaced," Jim called as he went through the glass doors to the back.

"Go ahead and try!" Lacey yelled back.

*

Chapter 14

Penny was excited about the arrival of Sarah and Dave, but realized she needed sleep. She took a couple of over the counter sleep aids and warned Jim to leave her alone.

"I have no intentions of attacking you tonight. I'm out of sorts, also. So, we will just crawl into bed and sleep."

"Good. Now, is the guesthouse ready for their arrival?"

"I checked and it was clean. I left a couple windows open to air it out. It hasn't been used since Angelo lived there."

"It doesn't smell like a mob enforcer lived there, does it?"

"That's unfair to Angelo. He doesn't have a mob enforcer smell. I wouldn't even know what a mob enforcer would smell like, and the guesthouse has no unusual smells. Other than being musty from being closed up."

"Good, I want Sarah and Dave to have a pleasant visit."

"They will if you leave them alone," Jim said under his breath, but Penny heard and whacked him. "Hey!"

"I'm not going to bother them. They are on vacation and here to get remarried, so I shall make their stay as pleasant as possible."

Jim's cell phone buzzed and he picked it up from the bed stand. "Excuse me, I'll take this out in the kitchen so you can sleep." He stood and went out of the bedroom. He looked at the caller ID, it said Warren. "Hey Greg, what have you found?" he answered.

"Larry ran it through his mass spec and said the lotion contained the same lead as in the sunblock. Not as much, luckily for Lynn. There were no prints on the tube other than Lynn's and Deacon's. They came up since they were in the cop database. The label gave us nothing, it was a fake company. I had them run the distributor phone number we got from Lyons' phone and it came up as a burn phone. We're nowhere unless we get some of the distributors to come in with the product and maybe we'll get some more info from them."

"Has anyone returned the product to the police?"

"Actually, we got four women who came in with boxes of the sunblock. They gave us names and addresses of customers who bought from them. We have men out looking for those people. I think we headed this off for now. But I need to know how Lynn got this tube?"

"After she woke, we asked and she said it came through the mail as a sample. I think since this went through the Post Office, it's now a federal crime. Will you call the feds in?"

"I'd rather not right now unless this gets sticky. I'll keep that thought in mind. Will you be around tomorrow?"

"Penny and I have house guests coming in from Washington State, so we'll be busy. I'll try and keep in touch, just to keep up on this."

"Thanks, I'll talk to you tomorrow some time." They said their goodnights and hung up. Jim went back into the bedroom and found Penny snoring lightly. He smiled and crawled into bed. He hoped he would sleep as well.

"What are we going to do now?" the man asked his partner. The two men stood in a small warehouse east of Las Vegas, surrounded by tables covered with fixtures to pump liquid into jars. There were a number of boxes stacked nearby all labeled 'Lotion' and most were now opened. The talking man waited for the other man to come up with an answer.

"I didn't figure they would catch on so quickly. It would have been a matter of time for them to associate the sunblock with the illnesses, but this was faster than I expected. We need to turn their attention to other dangers. Come with me." The man led the other man to a small office off the main warehouse. The room was sparsely furnished with only a desk and two chairs. They hadn't planned on making this a permanent base of operations.

"We need to divert the police's attentions to a new problem," the man said as he lifted a small box from the desk and opened it. Inside were four small hypodermic needles, each filled with a yellowish liquid. "We will go to a couple drug stores and then take these hypos and inject various lotions and creams with the liquid in the needles. Be sure not to be seen and make sure the puncture holes from the needles aren't obvious." The man picked up another box from the desk and handed it to his partner. "You go down Flamingo Road. There's a couple of drug stores around Spenser

Street. I'll head up the Strip. We'll meet back here. Don't get caught."

The men left the building to start their plan.

~~*~~

Jim was just finishing getting dressed when he heard a scream. He rushed out to the living room and saw the front door open. He went and looked out, finding two women hugging and bouncing around on the lawn. He smiled as he watched Penny and Sarah greet each other.

Jim went out onto the porch and found Dave standing in the drive, avoiding the women. Jim waved to Dave and motioned him to come up on the porch. He did and they shook hands.

"I won't hug you," Jim said.

"Thanks, I appreciate that," Dave replied.

"You're early. We weren't expecting you until noon."

"Sarah was up way too early and wanted to get moving, so here we are. I don't argue with her when she has a goal. Even if I'm still half asleep."

"Well, you made it safely," Jim said as the men watched the women giggling and talking. "I wonder what goes on in their heads?"

"I don't even try to figure it out," Dave said.

"Where's Van Gogh?"

"Oh, yeah, come with me," Dave said and went to his car. He arrived to the back door of the white Range Rover.

"Is this a new vehicle, and do you usually go on vacation in a Sheriff's car?"

Dave laughed as he opened the door, letting the dog out. Van Gogh headed straight to the bushes and began sniffing. "This became a replacement for our old patrol car. It's actually my personal vehicle, I bought it for my use, but I use it so much more for sheriff duties, I had the decals put on it." He pointed to the driver's door with a star above the word Sheriff, and below that, in smaller letters, it said Jefferson County, Washington. "I can write it off on my taxes that way."

"Did you remove the flashers?"

"They're in the back, in case I have to chase any bad guys," Dave said with a laugh.

Jim heard Willy yipping at the door of the house. He excused himself from Dave and went to let Willy out. The tiny dog shot right over to Van Gogh, who hadn't seen the dog yet. Willy stopped and yipped again, causing Van Gogh to jump and back off. They sniffed each other then ran around the yard, Willy chasing Van Gogh.

Dave came up to Jim. "Van Gogh is afraid of most things, other than serial killers. He's good to have around when we're in danger."

"Willy has saved us a few times. Good to have a dog. Cats would let us get murdered and not care."

"Very true," Dave said as they watched the women go to the house and in the front door.

"We better follow before they start rearranging furniture," Jim said. Jim called to Willy and he came running, followed by Van Gogh. Dave grabbed on to his dog's collar and led him behind Jim, now carrying Willy.

"Is it all right to bring Van Gogh in the house?"

"Sure, he's welcome. Let him run loose, Willy will keep him busy." They went in and found Penny and Sarah at the snack bar looking at Penny's laptop. Jim caught a glimpse of wedding dresses. "We better go to my office before the girls need us to give our opinions."

Dave laughed and followed Jim down the hall. They entered Jim's home office and sat. Van Gogh was sniffing around the room, Willy was sniffing Van Gogh.

"So, how's life in the woods?" Jim asked.

"About the same." Dave replied. "It's been pleasant since we haven't had any murders or abductions in a number of months."

"I heard about your flying saucer incident with the President of the U.S. and how you saved his butt."

"That was a weird experience. You've been busy here, too."

"Well, between mob hits, murderous Santas and Halloween killings, it's been fairly quiet lately. But if it wasn't, I'd have nothing to write about."

"How are the book sales doing?"

"Slow, but I'm not worrying about it. They go up and down with the seasons."

"Working on any big cases right now?" Dave asked.

"As a matter of fact, we have a case that has been a small nightmare. Seems someone is poisoning sunblock with lead and it's making people sick or causing them to die."

"Lead? Tetraethyl lead by chance?"

"Yeah, how did you know?"

"We had a plant up our way that was manufacturing the stuff for gasoline companies years ago. Many of the workers would get really sick from the stuff, but the company was greedy about profits and kept the people working. After the big bruha about the dangers of the lead in our environment, the plant closed down. Lots of workers still had ailments from the lead. Many died. Do you know where this lead is coming from?"

"No, we don't even know who is doing this yet."

"Well, I know where they may have been getting the lead from."

*

Chapter 15

"Really? Talk to me," Jim said.

"There's a concrete toxic waste dump below us that was supposed to be covered over with tons of cement, but the project was delayed due to the companies involved filing for bankruptcy. There are hundreds of barrels of Tetraethyl lead liquid. The EPA was supposed to do something about it, but so far politics and money got in the way. The stuff is covered with huge tarps to keep the rain from rusting the barrels, but in the climate around that area of Washington, it's always moist. I've heard rumors that someone has been stealing barrels, a little at a time. It's not in our jurisdiction, so we haven't investigated."

"Are there other places that made this stuff?"

"I heard of three other companies around the country, but they used up all the stock they had before they were shut down. So I'd say it was a good bet your lead came from our dump."

"I'll let the investigating detective know about this. Maybe he can trace it back there."

"I'm sure there has been no record of shipments of this stuff, so it may be difficult. It's like drugs, you don't put on record the delivery of tons of marijuana."

"Isn't weed legal in Washington now?"

"It is, and so far it's been no problem around my neck of the woods. I know where there are a couple weed farmers now, but we don't bother them, since the change in the law."

"Well, the lead situation has caused problems here. This is Vegas and sunblock accounts for a lot of sales. So far it's only been home distributors selling the stuff, nothing in the stores. I hope they don't start causing the same problem that spiking Tylenol did years ago."

Jim looked to the door when he heard voices coming down the hall. Penny and Sarah appeared at the door.

"We came to apologize for not saying hello. We got swept away by seeing each other," Penny said.

They all exchanged greetings and Penny asked, "What are you two plotting?"

"We were talking crime and lead poisoning," Jim said.

"Lead poisoning?" Sarah asked.

"Yeah, sunblock being laced with dangerous lead." Jim said. "We've had a few deaths caused by it in the last few days. You don't use the stuff, do you?"

"Around where we live, we're lucky to get enough sun to even burn.' Sarah answered. "I haven't used sunblock since I was living in New York and used to go visit the ocean. Do you have any leads on who's doing this?"

"No, it just started and there's not much evidence to use to find the people doing this."

"Let's talk about something more pleasant. Like a wedding.' Penny said. "Sarah and I have some plans started and need to know if Dave is inviting anyone to come and attend. I'm taking care of the travel and hotels."

"Well, Penny, that's real generous. I'll ask my deputies if they'd like to attend. I'm sure we can get fill-ins from the main office of the county sheriffs while they're gone. Sarah, are you going to invite Lois?"

"Only if I have to, she'll try and take over the whole thing. I'm going to see if Connie in New York can come out. I told Penny that I wanted her to be my maid of honor since I've known her for years."

"I'll see if Warren Stevens would be my best man, I've known him longer than anyone."

"Good, start calling all these people, we have a week to do this," Penny said. She looked at Sarah and said, "Shall we go visit Shelby Francis and see about the wedding gown?"

Sarah agreed. Penny said, "You two men can beat your chests over crime and murders. We have more pleasant things to do. Dave, call your people so I'll know who all is coming." The two women left the room.

"Now, we'll have some peace and quiet," Jim said. "You can use my desk phone to call your friends."

"I may as well use my cell phone. I'm on one of those unlimited plans, so may as well take advantage of it." Dave pulled his cell phone out and made the call. Ten minutes later, he hung up and said, "Virgil is more than happy to come out, Mike says he'll have to change a few things he had planned, he'll let me know. I think he just doesn't like traveling."

"You know, I'll have to throw you a bachelor party," Jim said with a grin.

"Is it going to be like that movie, 'The Hangover' or will it be tamer?"

"Dave, this is Vegas. We can get in all kinds of trouble."

"I'll be sure Sarah has enough cash to bail us out," Dave said with a laugh.

"No need, I'll have a number of cops joining us, so we'll be covered."

"How's the business doing? Still have Trapper, Buck and Earl with you?"

"Yep, they are. We keep busy with things like cheating spouses, missing husbands and the occasional murder. Feel like taking a ride to my office to meet a few new people?"

"Sure, what about the wives?"

"I'll leave a note, besides they'll be busy all day getting wedding arrangements made."

They stood and left the room. Jim wrote a note on the dry-wipe board in the kitchen and they went out to the car and headed to the office.

"I asked my friend Lynn about any openings in the Sheriff's department down here. You had mentioned it, last time I saw you."

"Thanks, but I'm happy where I'm at. This town is too busy. I've watched the 'Cops' TV show when they're in Vegas. It's too crazy for me."

"That's for sure. Occasionally when I get together with Deacon, Lynn and some of my cop friends, they talk about the funny things they all experienced. I've thought about writing a book about that."

"Jefferson County is fairly peaceful, except when we had that influx of serial killers and terrorists. I'm hoping we're back to normalcy."

"From what I saw of the country when Penny and I were visiting, I wouldn't mind having a cabin there to relax. I don't think I could move permanently from Vegas. This place gets under your skin."

They arrived shortly after, Jim pulled in and parked. "We have a large dog run, so we can put Van Gogh and Willy in there while we visit."

The back door opened and Fred came out with Henry, his dog.

Dave said, "Seems everyone has a dog."

"I'll introduce you to Fred, our handyman and night guard." They got out of the car and took their dogs to the cage.

"Fred, this is my friend, Sheriff Dave Chandler. He's from Washington State and here to get remarried to his wife."

111

Fred held out his hand to shake and said, "I heard Penny telling Lacey all about the wedding. It's going to be a big affair from what I heard."

"I hope it's not going to be too big. I just wanted to renew our vows."

"With Penny, everything is a production number," Jim said. He turned to Fred and asked, "Who all is in the building?"

"Trapper, Earl, Lynn, and Deacon. Buck said he was going back to Michigan, family emergency, or so he said."

"I hope it's nothing serious, strange he didn't call me about it," Jim said.

They put the dogs in the run and went in the building. Jim stopped at Earl's door but the room was empty.

"Everyone is up front," Fred said.

"Thanks," Jim replied and took them to the front. They came through the hallway to the front lobby door and out. They found everyone with Warren, talking.

"Jim, we didn't expect you to come in," Earl said. "Hey, Dave, how are you?"

"Good," he replied and greeted those people he met from the last time he was in town. Jim introduced Dave to Greg Warren.

"What's going on?" Jim asked.

"Greg came in to ask us if we knew of anything else from our investigation in the sunblock problem," Deacon said. "It looks like there may be another one."

"What?" Jim asked.

Warren spoke, "A woman bought some moisturizing cream from Rite-Aid Drugs on Flamingo and she applied the stuff to her hands and arms. She got the same symptoms that Lynn had and we were called from the hospital."

"Was it a brand name cream?"

"It was," Warren said. "When forensics examined the tube, they did find a small puncture hole where they say a hypo had to be inserted and pumped the liquid in the tube. This is a big problem now. We don't have the resources to check every tube or jar to see if these people are spiking good products now."

"What about store security cameras?"

"Forensics has the tapes from the Rite-Aid and is going through them. They hope to spot someone putting the lead into the products. We may need to put officers in the drug stores to keep this from happening further."

"Talk to Mac and see if they have extra guards that can watch the store customers."

"That's another reason I came in. Mac said he would pull in all his men who aren't active right now and get them into the stores. Unfortunately, there's a lot of stores, including grocery stores that sell beauty aids. I got with the media and they are going to put out a warning on the news. I just hope tourists in town don't buy this crap, and not see the news."

"Well, we may have one small lead," Jim said. "Dave mentioned that he might know where they are getting their supply of lead from. I'll let Dave explain."

*

Chapter 16

"Let's sit," Jim said motioning to the couches and chairs in the waiting area. They all sat and looked at Dave as he spoke.

"Well, there was a company up our way in Washington State, that made the liquid lead that was used in gasoline, but they closed up after the government put the ban on lead in our car's fuel. This company closed but they still had a large stock of the liquid in barrels that they had to dispose of. Local officials didn't want them to just dump the stuff, so they made a cement bunker and put the barrels in. They were going to cover the barrels with more cement but ran out of money. So the barrels sit in a big concrete hole covered in tarps. I've heard that there were barrels coming up missing, but the authorities out that way had no idea who took them. I think they may have ended up in your sunblock."

"Can you give me the names of the authorities to call about this?" Warren asked.

"Be glad to, I'll give them to Jim and he can get them to you."

"Works for me," Warren said, then stood. "I have to get back and organize the attack on this. Jim, have Mac call me for a list of places to put his men."

Jim nodded and said, "I don't envy you." He looked to Deacon and Lynn and said, "Why don't you two give him a hand in finding these criminals?" Jim knew that Warren liked to have help. Warren was a good detective but he was a little unsure about his abilities. Jim and Deacon had helped him a number of times in the past. Now that he was left behind in the squad, he had to survive on his own.

Deacon knew this also and said, "Be happy too, if Boering doesn't get upset."

"I'm sure Weber would be glad to have the two of you helping, screw Boering," Warren said with a grin.

Lynn stood and said, "Let's roll, this poison isn't going to go away."

They all said their goodbyes and left. Trapper said he was going back to his office to call Sam and let her know about the new warning. Earl said he had a spouse to follow and went to his office, leaving Jim and Dave alone in the lobby.

"Hi Dave," Lacey called from behind the counter.

"Lacey, Jim hasn't fired you yet?" Dave said as he stood.

"He couldn't replace me if he tried," she laughed and went back to her desk.

"Let's go to my office and relax," Jim said.

Penny and Sarah had arrived at Shelby Francis' Bridal Boutique and were browsing through all the wedding gowns. Sarah had chosen one from the photos Penny sent her and they were waiting for Shelby to bring it out.

"I had a small wedding for my first marriage." Sarah said. "Nothing fancy, we didn't have much money at the time. After my husband was murdered, I thought I would never get married again. It was about a year after that I met Dave and I had to start dating again or wither away as an old maid."

"You hardly are an old maid. I wish I was your age again," Penny moaned.

"For a woman in her sixties, you look great. I hope I look as good as you when I get to your age."

"It's just luck and good genes. I don't do much other than swim a lot. I'm not big on exercising, and I don't go in for fad foods. I walk a lot, which they now say is as good as exercise."

"But your face and skin is so beautiful, do you do something for that?"

"I clean and moisturize, but that's all, and I use good facial products. Nothing from the bargain stores. Now that we have a deadly poisoning going on, I'll have to ration out my creams until they catch the criminals."

"What's wrong with people to put lead poison in skin creams. It makes no sense."

"Well, soon the bad guys will announce their purpose for doing this. They always do. It's an ego thing, to beat their chests and tell their deranged story. Hopefully the police will catch them. With Jim and his men helping, of course."

"I'm sure Dave will love to help. He gets off on all this crime stuff. He complains about it, but I can tell he loves it."

"You two have been through the mill with serial killers and terrorists. I read two of your books about the incidents. Good books by the way."

"Thank you, but Jim is the real true-crime writer. I love his books."

"Make sure you tell him that. He's had a few bad reviews lately and it bothers him. Hearing something good, helps."

Shelby came through the open door from the back carrying a bag. She hung it up on a rack and unzipped the bag. Penny and Sarah came closer to see.

"I hope this is what you want. It's such a lovely gown." She said as she pulled back the bag to reveal the gown. Penny and Sarah helped her to remove it.

Penny and Shelby held the gown open to show Sarah. She smiled and said, "It's beautiful. Penny, I know this isn't going to be cheap, so I really appreciate you doing this for me."

"Don't flatter yourself, I'm doing this for me." Penny laughed out loud. "I never had a daughter to help with a wedding, so this is my vicarious thrill. Are your parents still around, are you inviting them?"

"No, both of them have passed on, auto accident years ago. My mother would have been your age, so you can substitute for her," Sarah said with a smile.

"Be glad to," Penny said. "Now let's get this gown fitted."

~~*~~

The LVPD homicide squad room was a bustle of activity. Weber was pacing around watching the men making phone calls to people who had bought the sunblock from the home distributors. Boering was trying to look official giving orders to men already doing their jobs.

Warren walked in with Deacon and Lynn in tow and he went straight for Weber.

"Greg, do you have anything?" Weber asked, then he saw Deacon and Lynn. "I certainly hope you two are going to help get to the bottom of this."

Lynn spoke first, "We're offering our services, if that's all right with you."

"Most certainly, good to have you both helping." He turned to Boering across the room and yelled, "Boering, you are to cooperate with Lynn and Deacon, you hear?"

Boering mumbled something to himself, then said loudly, "Will do, Captain. Glad for the help."

Weber turned back to Warren and asked again, "What do you have?"

Warren stood tall and said, "I have information as to where the lead is coming from and I'm going to follow up on it. I have extra security guards from Buck Carson's guard service that will patrol the beauty counters and aisles of a number of stores to watch for perps spiking cosmetics. I'm going to get with the electronic lab to see what they got from security cameras in the Rite-Aid store where the one poisoned cream was purchased."

"Very good, Greg. Fine job, keep me informed. Good to see you two," he said to Lynn and Deacon. "I have some work to do." He went back off to his office.

"He called you by your first name," Lynn said. "That's good."

Warren grinned, "Okay, where do we start?"

Deacon said, "Greg, where should we start?"

Warren thought a moment and then said, "Let's go see what they got off the videos."

"That's good, let's go." Lynn said and they left the squad room. Boering was not smiling as they left.

Down in the lab area of the precinct where they had all the CSI and forensic work done, they came to the electronic lab. Warren entered and was greeted by Larry the supervisor of the labs.

"Greg, we ran through the videos a couple times and found one person who was tagging a couple products. We managed to get a halfway decent facial photo from him. He wasn't very clever about it. Makes me wonder what kind of perps these people are."

Larry signaled to the tech at the computer and he brought up a photo image with info on the side. "The perp is named Manny Finnerman. He's a petty thief and mugger, with a record of breaking and entering. I can't see him being the mastermind behind this. He had to be a hired hand to take care of the grunt work. He probably wouldn't squeal on his bosses if we caught him."

"Well, we'll put a BOLO out on him and I'll get arrest warrant issued. He's involved in murder now, so he's moving up in the ranks of crime." Warren asked for a couple printouts and thanked Larry.

They went back towards the squad room when they came upon Weber and Boering in the hallway.

Warren spoke quickly, "Captain, we've identified one of the perps spiking the products with poison." He handed Weber the printout and waited.

"Great, get on this and bring him in," Weber said and went down the hall leaving Warren and Boering standing face to face.

"If you think you're going to get my job, think twice," Boering growled.

"If you did more than just give orders and prove you can do the job, then you shouldn't worry," Warren replied and walked around him heading to the squad room. Lynn and Deacon waited.

"You know Boering, I've never liked you," Lynn said. "As a matter of fact no one likes you." She went off following Warren.

Deacon just smiled and said, "Ditto." Then followed Lynn.

*

Chapter 17

"I called Sam and warned her about the new development in poisoned creams. She's letting her girls know about it. These people need to be stopped." Trapper said as he entered Jim's office.

"I just talked to Warren and he has a photo of the perp in the store spiking the creams. He's sending it by email. I'll print out a bunch of the photos to give to Buck's men before they go out to the stores."

Trapper sat and said, "Sometimes you feel so helpless in this business. Not knowing where these thugs are who are randomly killing people. Not even seeing their faces as they die. We need a crystal ball."

"If people had crystal balls, we'd be out of business," Jim said, with a laugh.

Jim turned to his computer and opened the email from Warren. He printed out the mug sheet and handed a couple to Trapper and Dave. He ran off a bunch more to give to the security guards.

"Is Warren going to pick this guy up?" Trapper asked.

"He told me on the phone earlier that they went to his last known address, but were told he moved. Of course, he left no forwarding address. So it's a matter now of watching for him. Hopefully, he'll try spiking more creams and they'll catch him."

"With security guards and cops watching the stores, they may back off for now. Maybe they'll go to a grocery store and poison some fruit or vegetables." Trapper said.

"Let's not get ahead of ourselves. Even if we were on the case, I wouldn't know where to start."

Trapper was reading the rap sheet on Manny Finnerman, and said, "It says here that he is related to Kenny Hooper, his cousin. I knew Kenny from my days on the force here, he's a punk, broke into houses and boosted cars. He liked to hang out at the Last Pocket Pool Hall on Decatur. Maybe he still goes there?"

"We've got nothing going on, shall we go investigate?" Jim asked.

They looked at Dave, he grinned, "I'm game if you don't mind an old county sheriff tagging along."

"I wish I was as old as you," Jim said, grinning. "Well, let's go."

The three men stood and went out to Trapper's Jeep. Trapper knew where the pool hall was so he drove. Fifteen minutes later they arrived.

Jim and Dave took another look at the mug shot for Manny so they could identify him. "Too bad we don't have a picture of the cousin," Dave said.

"I know what he looks like. If he's here, I'll find him." Trapper said.

They went in and waited until their eyes adjusted to the dim lighting. Trapper wandered around looking for Kenny Hooper. He asked a couple men shooting if they knew Kenny. One man pointed to the back of the hall in a separate room. Trapper signaled to Jim and Dave to go that way.

They entered the smaller room and Trapper pointed to a table in the back corner where three men stood watching one thin, scruffy looking man shooting. "That's Kenny," Trapper said and went around the room to the table. Jim and Dave went around the other side and stood next to some big man in a cutoff t-shirt watching the table. Dave looked at the man, nodded and smiled.

"What's your problem, Slim," the man growled.

Dave brought out his badge and said, "That's Sheriff Slim to you."

The man glanced at the badge, turned, and left the room.

Jim leaned to Dave and said, "I think you upset him."

"That's all right. I didn't like his looks. So what's Trapper going to do now?"

"Eventually, kick the crap out of him if he doesn't cooperate."

They watched as Trapper came up behind Hooper, standing close enough to block the pool cue as Hooper brought it back to shoot. He blew the shot and turned to see who messed him up. "Hey, man, what's the deal?" he moaned, then went silent. He recognized Trapper.

"Hello, Kenny. Long time no see. How's the home invasion business going?" Trapper asked the man.

Jim and Dave came around the table just behind Kenny, as Kenny brought up the pool cue to hit Trapper. Jim reached out and grabbed the stick pulling it from the man's hand.

"Hey, what the hell? You got friends to protect your ass."

"I don't need help Kenny. I just need to ask you a couple questions. Are you going to be a nice guy and talk to me?"

Kenny stood silently glancing between the men surrounding him. "What's in it for me?" he asked.

"Saving your skin. I never liked you, Kenny. I'd prefer to beat the information out of you, but let's do this like men. Where's your cousin Manny?"

"Manny? Hell, I don't know where he's hiding out now. He moves around when he gets thrown out of any place he stays. Okay, last I heard he was crashing in some warehouse where he found a job at."

"Doing what?"

"I don't know, he doesn't tell me anything. I only hear from him when he needs money. He must be getting paid, he hasn't asked in a while."

"Do you happen to know what warehouse he was in?"

"He asked me for a ride to the place. I said I couldn't take him. He said it was on Decatur, near Warm Springs Road. I didn't want to take him anywhere. He's a pain in the ass."

Trapper just stood staring at Hooper. "What?" Hooper cried. "I told you everything I know. I'm not going to take heat for Manny."

Trapper reached over and grabbed a pool ball and slid it across the table, knocking the eight ball in the side pocket. "Looks like you scratched, Kenny. Be good and stay out of trouble."

Trapper nodded to Jim and Dave and moved around the room towards the exit. Out in the car they sat.

"There's too many buildings in the area he mentioned for us to try and find the right warehouse. Call Warren and let him know. They can do a canvas with patrolmen to see if they can find it."

Jim pulled his cell phone and called Warren. He explained what they found out and Warren thanked them.

"Now what do we do?" Trapper asked.

Jim grinned and said, "We have a wild bachelor party to plan, so back to the office."

~~*~~

"This is so great!" Sarah exclaimed. "I love this dress."

Penny was happy also, as it wasn't the most expensive one in the group, but she wasn't going to mention that to Sarah. "I'm glad you like it. It is beautiful."

Sarah spun around in front of the giant mirrors on the wall, admiring the gown.

"While you were in fitting, I made calls to arrange for transportation for your guests. I called Connie and she regrets that she won't be able to come, but she said she'll be with you in spirit."

"Well, then I need a new maid of honor. Do you feel worthy of the job?"

"I'd be offended if you didn't ask. Yes, I'll be more than happy to be your maid of honor." Penny beamed.

Sarah hugged Penny. "It's settled, then. I'm going to get out of this dress before I mess it up."

"You do that, and I'll call Jim to see who Dave has coming." Penny pulled her cell phone as Sarah went back to the dressing room. The phone rang a couple times, then she heard Jim answer.

"Party central," Jim said in the phone.

"What are you doing, sweetie?"

"Trapper, Dave and I are planning world domination."

"Ah, the bachelor party. Will there be strippers involved?"

"You know Trapper, he'll have a few around."

"Well, don't corrupt Dave. I don't want to plan a divorce party while they are here."

"I'll make sure Dave is on his best behavior."

"Will I have to divorce you?"

"Me? No, I'll be good too."

"Just don't let Sarah or me find out. And don't do a remake of the Hangover movie. If you lose the groom, I'll kill you."

"Did you call to tell me this?"

"No, I need some information on who Dave has invited to this shindig."

"I'll let you talk to him, hold on." Jim handed the phone to Dave, and then he and Penny talked about Dave's guests.

"Good, I'll arrange for transportation and give you the info. Then you can tell your friends," Penny said. They finished the call and hung up.

Sarah came back out in her jeans and blouse. "You make any clothes look good," Penny said.

"Thank you. I've noticed you only wear dresses, shorts or shifts. Do you own any slacks?"

"I have one or two pair for being in the woods camping, but in the city, you'll never see me in them. I like the feel of sun and wind on my legs."

"I'm sure you like having men ogle your great legs, too."

"That helps, also," Penny said with a grin. "The men are plotting Dave's bachelor party. Shall we go set some ground rules?"

"Sounds good," Sarah said. They told Shelby they were leaving and thanked her for the help. They left and went back to the office.

*

Chapter 18

Lynn and Deacon were standing at the opposite end of Warren's desk away from Captain Weber. He was talking to Warren about what the detective had found so far on the poisonings and was looking at the photo printout of Finnerman.

"I also got a call from Jim Richards and he said that Will Trapper had managed to track down a cousin of our suspect. The info they got was where Manny Finnerman could possibly be located. I have officers going to the area where he was last reported. Hopefully they'll find his hideout." Warren spoke, hoping Weber was in a good mood.

"Very good, Greg. I'll have our reserve officers called in to help in the search. I'll even call the Clark County Sheriffs in on this. We can't let these people get away with this." Weber smiled and looked at Lynn and Deacon. "I'm glad you two can help on this. " He turned and went off to his office.

"He called me Greg again. I guess he's warming up to me," Warren said with a big grin. "So, all we can do now is wait to see if they find Finnerman. I hope it doesn't take too long."

"If he's in that area, I'm sure your men will find him." Deacon said.

"I hope so. Boering has been giving me the eye since I got back. I hate that guy," Warren said with a frown.

"Don't let him get to you, Greg. He's a jerk and everyone knows it." Lynn said.

"Let's get out of here, just to get away from him. We may as well go to where the search is going on in case they find him or where he's hiding out." Warren stood and led them out of the squad room.

Boering was at his desk watching them leave. He reached over and picked up his phone and made a call.

~~*~~

"I hope there'll be no strippers at your party," Sarah said, as she and Penny entered Jim's office.

Dave smiled and said, "You're all the stripper I need."

"And don't ever forget it," Sarah replied.

Trapper stood and gave Sarah his chair, pulling over one for Penny.

"So, are you all planned out for the wedding?" Dave asked his wife.

"I have the most beautiful dress, but you'll see it next week. If I don't catch you with a stripper."

Penny looked at Trapper, "Are you planning on any strippers or hookers?"

"Me? I gave up on them years ago. I'm getting too old for that kind of action."

Jim laughed, "You never got any action. You always pimped out the women to your cop friends in the holding cells."

"I refuse to answer that as it may be true," Trapper grinned.

"So what's happening with the sunblock killers?" Penny asked.

"I like that moniker, sunblock killers," Jim said. "That's now the official name for them. Trapper managed to track down a cousin of one of the sunblock killers, and we have a general location of the suspect."

"So, why aren't you out hunting him down?" Penny asked.

"Well, the location was vague and there are lots of buildings in that area," Jim said. "I gave Warren the information we got and he's sending his troops out to hunt down our sunblock suspect."

"Maybe three more people would help. You, Dave and Trapper are the best people to find them," Penny said.

"I appreciate your confidence in us, but the cops have more authority to search buildings," Jim replied.

"That never stopped you before," Penny grinned. "You don't need a warrant to enter places. Just a little B&E and you got your killers."

The men laughed. Jim looked to the others and said, "I guess sitting around here isn't doing much good. Shall we go join the search?"

They all nodded in agreement and stood. "What are you women going to do now?" Dave asked.

Penny grinned and said, "Shopping, of course."

"Just don't buy any creams or lotions," Jim warned.

"Oh hell, no. We aren't ready to die before the wedding," Penny replied.

"Okay, I'll see you later," Jim said and kissed his wife.

Dave kissed Sarah and Trapper complained that he didn't have anyone to kiss. Penny jumped up, pulling Sarah, and they both kissed him on his cheeks.

"Hah! I got two kisses," Trapper laughed and followed Jim and Dave out.

Penny looked at Sarah and said, "The mall is now ours to attack!"

~~*~~

"Move it, Manny! We have to vacate this place, the cops are coming," the man said to Finnerman.

"How did they know where we were, Harry?" Finnerman asked.

"Your stupid cousin opened his mouth and now we have to run," the man named Harry said. "Get that barrel loaded on the truck. We'll have to leave a couple of them here, we can't carry them all. Now move, it's only a matter of time before they get here."

The two men rushed to load as much equipment as they could put in the big pick-up truck. They closed up the back of the truck and then Harry said, "You screwed up this operation. Being seen on the surveillance cameras and letting your cousin know where we were holed up. I warned you about screwing up." He pulled out a gun and fired a couple bullets into the man. Finnerman fell as Harry ran to the cab of the truck after pushing the button to open the overhead door. He drove out and went down the street away from the building.

~~*~~

Warren answered his cellphone and listened. "Thanks, we'll be right there." Then he hung up and told Lynn and Deacon the news. "One patrol car was in the area where they heard gunshots. They drove around and found a small warehouse with the receiving door wide open. They went in and found our suspect on the ground. He's barely alive, but not conscious. The officer reported that they found a couple barrels of Tetraethyl lead. We have our base of operations."

"No suspects other than Finnerman?" Lynn asked.

"He didn't say, just that the place looked cleaned out. Somehow they must have known we were searching for them in that area. It should be just around this corner." He turned on the street and saw four patrol cars parked out front of one building. The EMS unit was just turning from the other direction and pulled up.

Warren parked and the three of them got out and headed for the building. One officer saw Warren, Lynn and Deacon coming in the building through the big door. He went to them and said, "I'm Officer Schmidt, I was first on scene and found the suspect on the floor. I called for a bus and then called you."

"Thanks, Schmidt. There was no sign of anyone else?"

"No. It does look like they just left. Finnerman wasn't shot that long ago judging by the way he was bleeding out. My partner tried to stop his bleeding, while we waited." Schmidt pointed to a row of tables and boxes. "This looks like the place they were spiking the sunblock. There's a bunch of boxes of the stuff piled back there."

Warren, Lynn and Deacon went to the tables. The place had a bad smell from the liquid lead.

"Well, we forced them to move, at least. Unfortunately, we didn't stop them. They had to have been in a truck, so I'll call to have every truck stopped and searched." He went aside and placed a call.

Deacon looked at Lynn and asked, "How are you feeling? You came back awful soon after you were poisoned."

"I'm fine, a little tired but I'll survive. I want these bastards as much as anyone. I really thought I was dying in the hospital. Luckily we got there quickly. I didn't want to leave you and P.J. so soon before we saw our daughter get married."

"Married? She's barely two. Don't rush her to the altar." Deacon laughed and kissed Lynn on the cheek.

"Let's go outside, this smell is bringing back bad memories for me." Lynn said.

Warren finished his call and was examining the table with a few of the apparatus still left. "They must have been busy loading the sunblock judging from the number of boxes they left of the stuff." He said to Schmidt standing by. "Since they know that we know about the sunblock, this must be all they had. I'll find out who leased this building, it should lead us to whoever is in charge. Good work, Schmidt. Thanks."

Warren went out to where Lynn and Deacon were standing getting fresh air. "I called to have the roads watched for trucks that may have the rest of the supplies and I need to find out who leased this building."

Deacon pointed to a sign on the building with the information to lease the building. "Maybe they were just holed up here and didn't sign a lease."

"I'm sure whoever owns the building must have come by to check on it and would have seen squatters. I'll call and find out." Warren went off to make the call, using the phone number from the sign.

Lynn and Deacon watched the EMTs bring out the suspect on a gurney and put him in the ambulance. They drove off in a flurry of sirens and flashers as Warren came back over to them.

"The owner said he leased the building on a short-term to some guy named Harry Hallson. I got his home address but I have a feeling its fake. Can't hurt to go see."

They went to Warren's car and drove out.

Chapter 19

Warren was just leaving the area when they spotted Trapper's car. Warren signaled to them and they pulled over. Jim, Dave and Trapper got out and went over to Warren's car.

"What's up?" Jim asked.

"Lots of excitement," Warren said and explained what they had found. "We're heading to the last known address of our main suspect now, if you can keep up, you can follow me."

Trapper agreed and they all drove out. Warren had checked on the address through his LEIN computer and got the location. They arrived at the house shortly after.

"Let's be careful," Warren said. "I don't see a truck around the house, so they may not have come back here."

Warren led them to the front as Trapper, Jim and Dave stood back. Deacon and Lynn were up by the door with Warren and ready for anything. Warren banged on the door and stood aside. No bullets came through the door, so he reached over and banged again, yelling, "Las Vegas Police, open up!"

There was no response, so Warren asked everyone to spread out around the house and check it out. Half of them went to the right, the others left. They were looking in windows that didn't have the blinds pulled down.

They met up at the back of the house and Lynn looked in the kitchen window and said, "We have cause to enter now." She pointed to a woman lying on the floor.

Deacon brought up his foot and kicked in the door. Jim said, "You could have tried the knob."

Deacon smiled and said, "More dramatic this way." He entered and went to the body. "She's dead," he said.

"I'll call the ME, Joe Lang," Warren said and pulled his cell phone. "Carefully check to see if there's anyone else in the house."

They all drew their weapons and moved carefully about. Jim looked at Dave and said, "Dave, you stay with Warren. If you get shot, Penny will shoot me."

Dave smiled and agreed. The rest of them were checking rooms and calling out 'clear' as they found the rooms empty.

The house was completely searched and they found no one. Warren came in the living room and was looking at a couple photos on a shelf. He picked one up and saw it was the dead woman with a man.

"I wonder if this is our suspect?" Warren said.

Jim looked over his shoulder and said, "Take it out of the frame and see if there's writing on the back. Penny always notes our photos."

"Good idea," Warren said and pulled the frame opened. He slid the photo out and turned it over. Everyone waited as he was reading.

137

"Me and Harry at The Venetian after the show," Warren read aloud with a smile, "Well, we have a photo of our suspect now. I'll get this back and have it blown up and sent out."

Trapper said, "I found a jar of sunblock on the kitchen counter. She must have put it on. I wonder if good old Harry knew she was going to do it, or he had her put it on to see if it would kill. She's been dead in here for a while."

"Joe Lang will be able to determine that, I called and he's on his way. Let's get out of here so the forensic people can do their thing when they get here."

They all moved outside and waited for the ME and CSI to arrive. They were on the front lawn as a woman came up from the house next door.

"Is there something wrong?" she asked.

"Yes, ma'am. We're investigating a homicide," Warren responded.

"Homicide? I always knew that bastard would hurt Melody bad," the neighbor said.

"Please explain," Warren asked.

"Her boyfriend was an animal. He would get stinking drunk and beat on her. He even threatened me once when I tried to help her. He should be put down."

"Well, ma'am, we'll do our best." Warren said.

She turned as Joe Lang's coroner's van pulled up.

"Oh, no. Is Melody actually dead?" she asked.

"I'm afraid so. Did you talk to Melody much?"

"She would come to me when he was passed out. I would tell her to leave the bum, but she wouldn't. She was so dependent on him. It was one of those things where a woman gets too strung out on a man who is brutal. She wasn't a strong woman."

"Excuse me," Jim asked, "You didn't happen to buy or get a jar of sunblock from Melody?"

"As a matter of fact, I did. I haven't used it yet, I don't get out in the sun much."

Warren asked, "Could you go get the jar, and don't open it."

The woman went to her house as Lynn said, "She evidently doesn't watch the news."

"Or the newspapers, they ran the story also." Deacon said.

They waited, and then the woman returned with the same jar as the rest.

"You didn't open this at all did you?" Warren asked.

"No, I wasn't really interested in it. Mostly because that jerk boyfriend gave it to me and said I should try it. I just didn't trust him."

"It's good you didn't. This sunblock was poisoned, and would have killed you."

"Is that what happened to Melody?" the woman gasped.

"We're not sure yet," Warren said, just as Joe Lang came up.

"Well, the body has been dead for about four days, I'd say. I'll know better when I get her into autopsy. But I will say she was poisoned by the sunblock. She shows signs of skin poisoning. I'll let you know what I find." He turned and went to the van as his men were loading the body inside the black bag into the van.

"Oh, dear. You never know who you live next to, do you?" the neighbor said.

"Did Melody tell you anything about Harry Hallson?"

"Was that his name? She just called him Butch. I never knew." She paused. "Melody said he worked for some industrial chemical company, I heard her say they were called Astro Chemical. They made cleaners and solvents, she said. She always hated the smells he had on him from work."

"That's probably how he connected with the people who supplied him with the lead," Dave spoke now.

"True, but why was he doing this? There has to be a motive in this crime," Trapper said.

"We never got any manifesto saying why they were killing. Nothing to explain or take credit for this." Warren turned back to the neighbor and said, "What kind of car was Butch driving?"

"He had a pickup truck. One of those big ones with big tires. He was always shining it, like it was his pride and joy. It was silver and a Chevy. I remember that."

"You don't remember a license number?"

"No, sorry. I never saw the plates. But he had a big sticker on the back saying the south shall rise again. I always thought it was funny."

"Well, that will help in our search for him. Thank you so much. Please be on the watch for him if he comes back, and call me." Warren handed her his card. "Just don't go near him or talk to him. Stay in your house."

"I will, thank you," she said and went back to her home.

The CSI team was already going through the house and Warren asked the supervisor to let him know what they find. He turned to his friends and said, "Well, we're getting somewhere. I don't see how he could hide his truck now. I'll put out a BOLO on him and the truck. I need to get this photo to be copied to send out. It's a matter of time now."

"I think he's going to lay low for a few days to organize his next move." Jim said. "We don't know if he's alone in this. He may have a team of people helping."

"But if we take down the leader, the rest will fall too." Lynn said.

"Very philosophical of you, Lynn," Deacon said.

Jim laughed and said, "Still learning new words, Deacon?"

"Yes, and he gets annoying with them," Lynn said. "Some words even I have to look up to be sure he's not insulting me."

141

"Me? Never would I vilify you," Deacon said with a sheepish grin.

"That's not an insult," Jim said to Lynn.

"It better not be."

They decided to follow up on the company that Harry had worked for, Astro Chemical. Jim checked the Google on his phone and got the location. They all went to their cars and drove there. They parked in the front visitors parking and went in. The six of them made an impression on the secretary.

"Well, how may I help all of you?" she asked.

Warren flashed his badge and said, "What can you tell us about Harry Hallson?"

"For starters, he doesn't work here anymore. He was fired last week for forging documents to have chemicals delivered outside the building. We handle dangerous chemicals and none are supposed to go anywhere but in the building under close watch. The supervisor didn't know he had chemicals delivered to an outside address."

"Do you know what kind of chemicals they were?" asked Warren.

"No, I don't, but you can ask his supervisor. I'll call him." She made a call and after a few moments a man came out. Warren explained that he needed information about Harry Hallson. The supervisor told them about his firing and why.

"What chemicals were involved?" Warren asked.

"Methol Ethyl Ketone. A powerful solvent. But that's what the shipping bill of lading said. I don't think that's what was shipped."

"Can you tell us where the shipment came from?"

"He ordered it from a company in Washington State."

*

Chapter 20

Jim looked at Dave, "Seems you were right about the chemicals coming from your area. I hope Warren can use the info you gave him to track the company down."

Warren asked the supervisor, "How was he able to order chemicals from this company in Washington?"

"We deal with a number of companies, so it was no big deal to place an order for just about anything," the supervisor said.

"Does anything cover Tetraethyl Lead?" Trapper asked.

"Tetraethyl lead? No, that was banned years ago as a gasoline additive. I wouldn't have any idea how he would get hold of that chemical."

"What company was the order placed through?" Warren asked.

"Stile's Chemical. I talked to them and they said they didn't have any orders from us recently. I gave them the order number and they looked it up. The man I talked to was surprised to find there was an order for Methol Ethyl Ketone made, but he didn't know how it was made."

"What did his order say? How many barrels of the stuff were shipped?" Jim asked.

"He said according to his shipping order, that six barrels were sent out, but he went to check and he told me that they weren't short six barrels of the ketone chemical. He couldn't explain it."

Warren turned away from the man and said to Dave, "Do you know any authorities in that area who can investigate?"

"No, but since banned chemicals were transported across state lines, I have a friend in the FBI who would love to check on it." Dave said. "As a matter of fact, I invited him to my wedding, so he'll be here soon."

"Good, we need to get on this," Warren said and then turned back and asked, "You say six barrels of the stuff were sent. Where was the shipment sent to?"

The supervisor went to the computer on the secretary's desk and started to hit keys. He spent a few minutes hunting for the invoice and then finally found it. "I'll print out the order for you."

"Thank you. Does it say the shipment came to Las Vegas?" Warren asked.

The man looked at the screen. "Yep, it was delivered to an address just outside the city." He reached down and pulled a paper from the printer and handed it to Warren.

Warren was reading the sheet as Trapper and Jim were trying to look over his shoulder. "There's an address here, but it's not familiar to me. I guess we need to pay a visit." Warren thanked the man and went out followed by his friends.

Deacon and Lynn said they were going back to the office. "We should go see if there's any new cases coming in. Can't have all the investigators hanging together."

"Good idea. Call if there's anything big," Jim said. "How are you getting back? You came with Warren."

Trapper spoke, "I'll take them. I want to go back and call Sam to see how she's doing."

Jim asked Warren, "Do you mind if Dave and I go with you?"

"No, I'd welcome it. Let's go."

Trapper drove off with Deacon and Lynn as Jim and Dave got into Warren's car.

"Where are we going?" Jim asked.

Warren handed Jim the sheet of paper, "Here, Mr. Geography. Navigate us to the place."

Jim got on his cell phone to the Google map program and found the location for the address. He told Warren where to go.

They drove out of the city until they found the factory where the barrels were delivered. The building was rundown and looked closed. The fence and gate was rusting and falling down.

"Well if the barrels were delivered here, someone had to accept them. I wonder why the delivery people didn't wonder why they were bringing the barrels to a closed down factory," Jim asked.

"Let's explore since we are here. Might find something to give us a lead," Warren said as he got out of the car.

The men went through the broken gate and up to the building. Jim was looking around the ground.

"There's tire tracks that look recent, and tracks from the barrels. They weren't taken in the building, but there are other tracks over here where the barrels were rolled to. So this was just a dump site for the delivery," Jim said.

"I'll have CSI come and get tire impressions to see if we can identify the trucks," Warren said. "Let's just look inside to see if they camped out waiting for the delivery."

They went up to the front glass doors and found it locked. They looked through the glass and the floor had a coating of dust and dirt. "No sign of movement in here, the dust on the floor wasn't disturbed," Warren said. "Maybe they hung out in the truck. I'll call in CSI." He went down away from the building to place a call.

"What was the name of that company in Washington where the barrels came from?" Dave asked Jim.

146

"Stiles Chemical, was what he said," Jim replied.

Dave pulled out his cell phone and pushed a couple buttons. He held the phone to his ear and waited. "Virgil? This is Dave," he said. "Yes, Virgil, Sheriff Dave. How many Daves do you know?" He waited for an answer, then smiled. "I need you to look up a company. Get with the main Sheriff's office and see if they can help. Look up a company called Stiles Chemical and find out what you can about them. Especially any illegal activities involving chemicals." He paused to listen, then, "Yes, Virgil, we're going to investigate the company. So find out what you can and call me." He hung up before Virgil could say anything more. "Virgil is a good man, handy, but a little slow in the gray matter," Dave said to Jim.

"I understand. I've dealt with a few people like that. Do you think he'll find anything?"

"Virgil has always wanted to be a P.I. so this will stimulate him. I'm sure he'll find out everything about them."

Warren came back. "CSI will be out shortly." Jim told Warren about Dave's call. "Good, I hope he can find something about the company. If they are dealing in banned chemicals, hopefully we'll know."

They went back to the car and stood waiting. "Greg, you know I'm getting remarried next week, have you been invited?"

"Jim mentioned it, I'd be happy to come. I presume there will be a bachelor party?"

"Of course," Jim said. "But you will be sworn to secrecy as to where it will be and who will be attending."

"Strippers?" Warren grinned.

"We'll see," Jim replied slyly.

A few minutes later the CSI team pulled up and Warren went to explain what was needed. They went to the tire tracks and examined them, then prepared to make casts of the best tire impressions.

"They should be able to get a make of the tire and what trucks they are put on. I'm always amazed how they can do this," Warren said, standing at the fence watching the men work on getting the cast.

"We use the forensic people from Olympia Headquarters for the Sheriffs," Dave said. "I've been to their labs and it's is amazing the technology they have."

"Harry Hallson had a pickup truck. Do you think one set of those tracks could be his?" Jim asked.

"All we know is it was a big silver Chevy. Although the neighbor woman said it had big tires. I'm assuming they were oversized. I'll go mention it to the Supervisor." Warren went back to the CSI and talked to them as Jim and Dave waited.

Warren came back just as Dave's cell phone rang. He looked at the caller ID and said, "It's Virgil. Maybe he has something for us."

"Can you put it on speaker?" Jim asked.

Dave nodded and answered, "Go ahead Virgil, what do you have?"

Virgil's voice came out of the speaker. "I called the area commander and asked about the company. He told me they had a number of problems with Stiles. Seems they were shipping various chemicals out of the country to South America. Something to do with drug manufacturing. Stiles managed to beat the charges, but the Feds have been watching them."

"I'll call Warren Stevens and ask if he knows about the FBI watching them," Dave said. "Can you find out anything about that toxic dump with all those barrels of that gasoline additive, the Tetraethyl lead stuff? The one south of Brinnon."

"I'll get right on it," Virgil replied.

"Did you get my message about the plane flight down here for the wedding?"

"I did, and I'm real stoked up to hit Sin City."

"Yeah, well, don't get in any trouble down here. The local police don't mess around," Dave said with a smile to Warren.

"I'll be good, Dave. I'll check on the dump and get back to you," Virgil said and hung up.

"I wonder if Hallson's ex-supervisor knows that the company he deals with is shady?" Warren asked.

"He didn't seem concerned about the company when we spoke to him. Either he knows and doesn't care, or he doesn't know." Jim said.

Warren's cell phone rang, he answered, listened, then hung up. "That was Williams, he said they found Hallson's truck, burned out down in Jean, Nevada. The county Sheriff's reported the truck from our BOLO."

"Where is Jean, Nevada and what's there?" Jim asked.

"It's about 32 miles south on I-15," Warren replied. "The only thing down there besides the Gold Strike Gambling Hall is the Jean Airport. Maybe Hallson was taking a flight out of the state."

"Feel like a nice ride in the desert?" Jim asked Dave.

"I'm game," Dave replied.

*

Chapter 21

Dave was in the backseat of the unmarked car, watching out the window at the miles of open land. "Pretty desolate out here. I'm used to trees and lots of green up in Washington State."

"Las Vegas used to be lush and green way back around the time the Mormons moved in. The name Las Vegas means 'The Meadow' and it dried up by the time settlers started to take over from the Native Americans."

"Same old story. White man takes and gives nothing back," Warren said.

"Now the Native Americans have gambling casinos and they're taking the white man for his money," Jim said with a laugh.

"Serves them right," Warren said.

"Greg, are you championing the Native Americans?" Jim asked.

"I'm in a small part Native American, on my mother's side. I heard all the tales from my grandparents about the treatment their ancestors got from the white settlers. It's disgraceful."

"Well, they're taking it back now. How much longer to Jean?" Jim asked.

"About two more minutes. There's the sign." Warren pointed to the city limit sign and drove on.

"I'd say by the smoke, we found the truck," Jim said as he pointed to a small plume of black smoke still rising in the distance. "When did the fire begin?"

"Williams didn't say if it was out or still burning."

"Could be the tires, they take a while to burn. Hard to put out," Dave said from the back.

Warren pulled off the road to where he saw the fire trucks and men working on putting out the last of the fire. Black smoke was coming from the truck as the firefighters hosed it down.

Warren showed his badge to the fire chief and asked how long it had been burning.

"Someone doused it in an accelerant that was hard to hose down. All we can do is keep it contained until it burns out."

"How did you know this was the truck we were after?"

"License plates. I called the Sheriffs to give them the plate number. They found it on your BOLO. I'm surprised that they didn't remove the plates. Excuse me, I have to go play chief." He went off as Warren turned to Jim and Dave.

"I'm wondering if Hallson deliberately did this to get us off track. Burn out the truck and head back to Vegas. While we are screwing around down here, he's up poisoning more products," Warren said.

"I'm agreeing with that. Now what?"

"I'll have our forensics haul the truck back to the lab and see if the tires match, first. Then, see if the fire didn't burn away all evidence." Warren went to the fire chief.

"This is getting complicated. We're doing a lot of running around," Jim said.

"You don't have any definite evidence that points to the bad guys, so most of this is slowly leading to them," Dave replied.

"Yeah, but it would be nice to know where they are."

"Then the case would be over and we can concentrate on the bachelor party."

Jim laughed as Warren came back. "The fire chief is going to keep the truck safe until CSI can come get it. Let's go back."

On the way back, Jim said, "I'm wondering, the neighbor woman said that Hallson spent a lot of time polishing the truck. It's strange he would torch his beloved vehicle."

"He must be worrying about something. Maybe he knows we are getting closer to him. We know his name and it's just a matter of time before we find him," Warren said.

"I'm wondering if Hallson is alone in the poisonings? Is he the mastermind or just following orders from some unknown person?" Dave offered.

"Good point. We won't know until we find Hallson, hopefully soon," Jim said.

Dave's cell phone rang and he answered, "Yeah, Virgil, what do you have?" He listened for a moment and thanked the man, then hung up.

"Virgil contacted the Sheriff's department in the county where the toxic dump was located and they said that the place was being pillaged at least once a month. They estimate that around twenty barrels have been taken, going by the original work orders to bury the site," Dave said.

"Well, Hallson only got six of the barrels according to his ex-supervisor. The others must be somewhere else around the country. I hope this poisoning thing isn't going to be country wide," Jim said.

They made small talk for the next ten minutes before they got back into Las Vegas. Warren drove back to Jim's office to drop them off.

"It's getting late and not much more we can do until they examine the truck. Hopefully they'll find something that will help," Warren said.

"I'll call you early tomorrow morning. We'll go from there. Thanks for the ride in the country," Jim said and closed the car door. Warren drove off as Jim turned to see Fred coming out the back door of the building. Jim and Dave went to Fred and introduced Dave.

"Yes, I've heard about you from Lacey. She seems to be a fountain of information," Fred said.

"Sometimes too much information. Who all is inside?"

"Deacon and Lynn are in the break room. Trapper is on the phone in his office. Earl is off on a case."

"Good to see someone is earning an income. Is Penny here?" Jim asked figuring Penny may have parked in the front.

"Haven't seen her, sorry."

"No problem, thanks." Jim took Dave in the building and to the front. Lacey smiled as they came through the glass doors.

"Hi Dave," she said.

"Lacey, you get more beautiful every time I see you," Dave replied.

"You saw her earlier today," Jim said.

"Well, she's better looking than before," Dave said with a grin.

"Leave him alone, Jim. He can compliment me anytime."

"Has Penny checked in?"

"She called to tell you that she and Sarah would be at the house swimming."

"Of course," Jim said with a laugh. "Your wife will be water logged before Penny is finished with her," he said to Dave.

"Sarah likes swimming in the Hood Canal behind our house. The water is too cold for me."

"Let's go see what the other great private investigators are doing in the break room." Jim led Dave to the door and in. Deacon was banging on the pinball machine as Lynn was watching him.

"Good to see that machine is getting a work out," Jim said as they approached.

Deacon lost the ball and backed away from the machine as Lynn took her turn. Deacon moved over to Jim.

"So any luck at the chemical company?" he asked.

"The place had been closed down for a long time. It was just a dump site for the chemical barrels. Our suspect's truck was found down in Jean, Nevada, burning."

"No sighting of him?"

"Nope. We think he took the truck down there and torched it as a diversion. It doesn't make sense to be running around in a truck that can be identified. He probably had someone bring him back here. Now we wait for the next round of poisonings."

Lynn lost her ball down the chute and the game was over. "There were no new cases coming in. Earl is the only person who has one."

"Well, hang in here until closing. I'm taking Dave to my house to see how badly our wives are water soaked," Jim said.

"Penny's in the pool again?" Lynn asked.

"Yeah, she hasn't used it much lately, so I'm sure she's making up for it. Talk to you guys later." Jim took Dave back out to the car and drove home.

~~*~~

Hallson was on the phone from the motel room he had holed up in. "Listen, I didn't like having to fry my truck. If they hadn't gotten that nosey neighbor telling them about it I'd still have it." He paused until the person on the other end finished speaking. "Yeah, I know this isn't the way it was supposed to go. You said the lead was only supposed to make them sick, not kill them. Hell, man, I'm now a murderer. All those people, I'll go away for a long time if I don't get the death penalty. You said you'd protect me, do it." He listened, then said. "I don't care how much pull you have with the police, you were supposed to solve this and take the credit. I was supposed to disappear while you took out Finnerman as the killer." Pause. "Yeah, I know I shot him, he was becoming a liability. You're letting that other cop take over the case, he'll find me, then what will you do?" More listening. "I'm getting out of here in the morning. I'll head south to Mexico before they can get me. This is your fault. I'm sorry I let you talk me into this." Hallson hung up on the other person.

"Damn, cops," he muttered. Then he pulled a sheet of paper from the desk drawer and started writing.

~~*~~

Penny took a big leap off the newly installed diving board into the deep end of the half-sized Olympic pool. Sarah sat on a chaise lounge watching and sipping on her glass of wine.

"Nice to see women can still have a good time," Jim said from the patio.

Sarah jumped hearing the men behind her. Dave came up and took the wine from her hand. "Just how much of this have you had," he said as he took a sip. "Ugh, that's too sour."

"It's imported and it will be served at our wedding," Sarah replied.

"I hope we'll have beer, also," Dave responded.

"If I have anything to say about it, we will," Jim said. "And chips, lots of chips."

"Who's arranging this wedding?" Penny said holding on to the side of the pool. "Beer and chips, you can have them out in the parking lot."

Jim looked at Dave, "That works for me."

*

Chapter 22

Penny came up out of the pool and went to Jim, giving him a big wet hug. "Well, that's refreshing," Jim said.

"So did you find your poisoner?" Penny asked.

"No, but we're getting closer. We know who he is and it's just a matter of time before we find him," Jim replied, sitting on a lawn chair. Dave sat on the end of the chaise lounge forcing Sarah to move her outstretched legs.

"Any more cases of death by poisoning?" Penny asked.

"No, it's been quiet. I think the killers have backed off for now since we are on to them. Hopefully they'll cease their operation. The police found their building where they were making the poisoned sunblock, but the killers took some of the barrels of lead with them. So they still could be dangerous."

"Could they dump the lead in the water supply to poison lots of people?" Sarah asked.

"Someone said that it would take a lot of the liquid lead to affect the people of Vegas through the water supply. They only were able to take three 55 gallon barrels when they left their warehouse, I don't think that would be enough to pollute the water supply."

"Still enough to do some damage in other ways," Dave said.

"Yep. I hope they just stop for now, so we can get on with the wedding," Jim said.

"You weren't hired by the police to help investigate, so you can just worry about the wedding and let the police handle it," Penny said.

"True. Dave and I have to finish planning the bachelor party. I have to see if we can rent one of those party limos." Jim stood and motioned for Dave to follow.

"Party limo? Just what are you up to?" Penny inquired.

"I'm going to show Dave how we party here in Las Vegas, especially for a wedding."

"Why? Weddings are being done at drive-through windows in town. Marriage is no big deal here. Everyone does it. You can get married here, then go up to Reno and get a quickie divorce."

"This is coming from the woman who wanted to duplicate the royal wedding of William and Kate. Where's your spirit of adventure?"

"I'm suspicious of what you are up to. If you ruin this wedding, I'll take a trip to Reno."

"I'll have Dave safely to the altar. Sober and standing." Jim laughed and went to the house followed by Dave.

"I just wanted a simple ceremony to renew our vows. I hope this won't become a circus," Dave said.

"Don't worry, Penny and I like to out-do each other with talk. We will have a nice wedding for you two. Don't worry. As for the bachelor party, it will be tame. Just a few of my friends and the ones you invited. When is your FBI friend, Warren Stevens, getting here?"

"He said Monday, so I'll need to be guided to the airport to pick him up. He's coming in with Virgil."

"No problem. Penny told me that your guests and Sarah's will be put up in the Luxor Hotel across from the airport. Does Sarah have any people coming out?"

"She hoped her friend Connie would come out from New York, but she has obligations to take care of. As much as she didn't want to, she asked her friend Lois to come down."

"Lois? Isn't she the person who introduced you to Sarah?"

"Yes, and she can be a pain in the butt at times. She's a good woman, just a little rambunctious," Dave said with a laugh.

They ended up in Jim's home office and sat. Jim took out a phone book and thumbed through it. "I have a mini-limo but it would be too small for the number of men I think we'll have. I'll see if they have a rental limo that can take us around town."

"Where will we end up in it?" Dave asked.

"I'll think of a few places to visit, all tame so the women won't have fits."

Jim wrote down the name and numbers of a couple limo rentals and closed the book. "Now to plan out our evening."

~~*~~

Hallson had returned from a trip to where the lead barrels were stored. He had to leave something with them. He came back in the cab and later was startled hearing the knock on his motel door. He wasn't expecting anyone, so he picked up his gun from the dresser and looked through the peephole. It was someone he knew. He opened the door and said, "What are you doing here, I thought we weren't supposed to be seen together?" Hallson said and put his gun back on the dresser.

The visitor pushed Hallson back and drew a gun from his coat. He aimed it at Hallson, who put his hands up in defense and said, "What the hell are you doing?"

The man went to the bed and grabbed a pillow, pushing the gun into it and fired twice at Hallson. The shocked Hallson fell back as the man went over him and fired once more to be sure his victim was dead. The man dropped the gun next to

Hallson, removing his gloves and put them in his pocket. He went to the door, opening it cautiously, looking around to be sure there was no one to identify him, then left.

Ten minutes later an anonymous call was made to the LVPD about gunfire at the Starlight Motel.

An hour later, Greg Warren was called to the motel. He went to the room where the police and Joe Lang, Clark County Medical Examiner, were hovering at the door while the crime scene people examined the room.

The detective in charge, Matt Frantone, remained stone-faced, a condition he usually expressed, as Warren came up.

"Matt, what's up and why was I called?" Warren asked.

"You were looking for the sunblock killer? Well, we found him," the detective said pointing to the body on the floor.

"So, he must have had a partner in this. Guess they had a difference of opinion." Warren said.

"We found a .38 Police Special next to the body. CSI took it in for ballistic check. The killer muffled the sound with a pillow."

"Who called it in?"

"Don't know. Anonymous call led us here. Found the door was left opened, someone wanted us to find him."

Joe Lang said his greetings to Warren and went in the room to examine the body. Warren and Frantone stood watching as Lang was checking over the body. He looked back to the men and said, "Two shots at close range to the chest and one more to the head. I'd say he was executed by a pro. Someone he must have known to get this close with a pillow over his weapon."

A half hour later, the body was removed and the room was cleared by forensics. Warren was looking around at the personal items left by Hallson. He and Frantone found nothing of usefulness to give them an idea of what Hallson was up to.

"I got the phone logs for the calls Hallson made and received. We may have something to go by with that," Frantone said.

"It's getting late, let's lock up here and wait to see what forensics has," Warren said. They closed up and put police tape over the door. "Thanks for the call, I wanted to find him, I really did, but not this way. Talk to you in the morning."

They went to their cars and drove out.

Early the next morning Jim was struggling to get out of bed. Too many beers last night with Dave had its consequences. Penny was nowhere to be seen, so Jim went out through the open patio doors, past the ugly Greek statue still pouring water in the Koi pond. Jim stopped and grabbed some fish pellets, throwing them to the huge goldfish. He watched them devour the pellets, then went around to the pool.

Penny and Sarah were each floating on the water, resting on inflatable mattresses. Penny looked over to Jim and said, "Good morning, sweetie. How's the head?"

"A bit huge from inside. Where's Dave?"

"He's still in bed. He's enjoying not having to get up early and go to work," Sarah said. "I let him sleep in when he has time off."

"I won't disturb him then. I need to put something in my stomach to balance my head." Jim turned and went back in to the kitchen. He was putting bread in the toaster when he heard his cell phone buzzing. He had left it in the bedroom, so he rushed to get it.

"Hello?" he said, not looking at the caller ID.

"Jim, it's Deacon. Did I wake you?"

"No. I was just making breakfast. What's up?"

"I got a call from Greg Warren. Seems they're looking at him for murder."

*

Chapter 23

"Murder? Who?" Jim said, as he went back to the kitchen. His toast had popped up, so he pulled the slices and put them on a plate.

"As I understand, they found Harry Hallson murdered in a motel room in the north end. The ballistics on the gun proved it was the murder weapon. The kicker is that the gun was registered to Greg. Feel like joining me to help him?" Deacon said.

"Of course. Give me about a half hour. Are you at the office?"

"Yeah, I came in to get some paperwork finished for Lacey, when Warren called my cell phone. He didn't know who else to call. Poor guy is really messed up by this. We'll get more when we talk to him."

"I'll see you there," Jim said and hung up. He went out and over to the guesthouse. He knocked on the door and waited. Dave finally opened and looked worse than Jim felt. "What's up?" Dave asked.

"Problem. Greg Warren has been accused of murdering our poisoner. I'm going to meet with Deacon and go see what's up. Feel like going along?"

"Yeah, give me a couple minutes to get dressed."

Jim went back to the house and found Penny and Sarah in the kitchen eating his toast. Jim had to smile, he wasn't really feeling like eating the toast. "Sure, finish my breakfast."

"Well, you weren't here and it was getting cold. Where were you?"

"Waking Dave up. There's a problem and I wanted to know if he wanted to go along."

"What problem?"

"Greg Warren is accused of murder. Deacon called me and I'm meeting him to see what we can do to help him."

"Yes, do what you can to help Greg. Tell us later what happened," Penny said.

Jim went to the bedroom to finish dressing then met Dave in the driveway. They got in Jim's Crown Vic and drove over to the office. They could see Lynn and Deacon in the parking lot as they pulled in.

"Jim, Lynn and I are heading to the precinct, follow us," he said and they went to their car.

Ten minutes later they were at the back door to the precinct and entered. The desk officer saw them and waved them through to the squad room. They entered homicide and saw Captain Weber talking to a person who Jim recognized. It was the prosecuting attorney for Clark County. This worried Jim.

The lawyer left, as Weber looked over and saw them, he smiled as they approached. "Deacon, Lynn, glad you're here. This is not good. Let's go to my office to talk."

As Weber took them to his office Jim looked back and saw Boering standing watching them leave. He had a strange smile on his face. Jim did not like that man.

"So, Captain, what happened?"

"Okay, as I understand it, Harry Hallson was murdered in his motel room. The gun that killed him was registered to Greg. It has his prints on it also," Weber said.

"Captain, you know Greg as well as I do. What motive would he have to kill Hallson?" Lynn asked. "He was trying to catch him."

"It was also found out that Hallson made numerous calls to this squad room. Prosecutor is claiming Greg and Hallson were working to together to commit these crimes so Greg could take credit for stopping the crime."

"Do you honestly believe that, Captain?" Deacon asked.

"When Boering was brought in to the squad, I could tell Greg was upset for being passed over as Lieutenant. This crime would be a feather in his cap for promotion."

"Who decided that was what happened?" Deacon asked, testily.

"Boering brought it up. He made sense in his theory of how Greg could have organized this with Hallson."

"I'm not believing this! Greg is not the kind of person, or cop, that would do this." Lynn was getting steamed. "Does Greg have an alibi for when the crime happened?"

"Unfortunately, he doesn't. He said he went back to the warehouse where the killers had set up a base of operations. He said he was looking for anything to explain why they were doing this. He was alone, no one to back up his story."

Jim mumbled, "This whole thing seems flimsy. Like some amateur is setting Greg up."

Weber looked at Jim and said, "Frankly, I agree." Weber suddenly saw Dave sitting behind Jim. "I'm sorry, but do I know you?"

Jim moved his chair over and said, "Captain, this is Sheriff Dave Chandler. From the Jefferson County, Washington Sheriff's office. He's a friend and he and his wife are in town to renew their marriage vows."

"Sheriff, eh? Well, welcome to Vegas," Weber said, then paused. "I remember you now. You helped take down those drug dealers when Penny and that other woman were held in the city by the drug cartel we busted."

"That other woman is my wife. Luckily, she survived her trip to Vegas unscathed," Dave said with a smile.

"Well, welcome back. Now we have to get evidence to prove Greg is innocent. I know Boering believes he did it, and Williams is not smart enough to solve a jigsaw puzzle. You guys get together with Greg and work this out." He sat back in his chair and then said, "The poisonings have stopped with the death of Hallson. We're still looking for the remaining barrels of the lead. Hopefully they are stored away out of the hands of anyone who can do harm with them."

"Believe me Captain, I want to see Greg cleared of the charges. We'll talk and see what we can do," Deacon said.

"Deacon, I'm officially assigning you and Lynn as consultants to the LVPD. You too, Jim. Greg is in room 2 waiting to be interrogated. I told Boering to stand off on this, and I put Williams in charge. You can get with him to talk to Greg." He looked to Dave, "Sheriff Chandler, I hope you can help also."

Dave nodding his agreement and then Weber stood. "Okay, go to work."

Everyone left the office and went down the hallway to interrogations.

"This whole thing is flimsy," Jim said again. "I'm not believing there's even a case here against Greg."

Lynn stopped and said, "Jim, there is a man dead and the gun that killed him belonged to Greg and he has no alibi. That's all the prosecutor needs to hold Greg for suspicion of murder. He's innocent, you know that and so do I, but in the eyes of the lawyers, he's guilty until proven innocent."

"Don't you just love jurisprudence? I still hate lawyers." Jim gave a fake smile and they went down to where Warren was being held.

They found Detective Williams standing outside the room where Warren was sitting in. "Lynn, Deacon, good to see you're here. I'm not sure about this case and I understand you were helping Greg with it. This is not good, we need to get him off of these charges."

"Let's go in and talk to him. Then we can go from there," Lynn said.

Williams opened the door and went in followed by Deacon and Lynn. Jim held back and said to Dave, "Let's go watch from observation."

As soon as Williams entered, he went to the side of the room to let Deacon and Lynn take the chairs across from Warren.

"Deacon, Lynn, I didn't kill Hallson. Why would I?" Warren pleaded.

"It's okay Greg, we're on your side, so let's go over this," Lynn said. "The gun was yours, how did it end up in the motel with Hallson being shot by it?"

"That gun was my extra backup piece. I always kept it in my locked desk drawer and after I heard about the charges, I checked. The drawer was unlocked and the gun was gone. Someone took it out."

"Who would have done that?" Deacon asked.

"I can't say but I have a suspicion that it was Boering. He threatened me the other day about taking his job. Of course I wanted the job but not enough to commit a crime for it."

"You said you went back to the sunblock factory, no one saw you?" Lynn asked.

"No, there was no one there. I thought that if I looked around, something would jump out about the reason they were doing this. It was funny, they

170

had the equipment to put the poison in the jars, but nothing else to point to why. There was no paperwork about their operation. It was almost as if they had one mission, to fill jars with poison and send them out to the public. I would have thought they would have some purpose to their actions."

"Was your desk drawer forced open to get the gun?" Deacon asked.

"No it was unlocked. Stupidly, I put the key in the back of my middle desk drawer, way in the back. I didn't tell anyone, but I guess if someone watched me they would know where I kept it."

"Has anyone touched your desk since you checked to see if the gun was there?"

"I don't think so."

"Bottom drawer?"

"Yeah, right side."

Deacon looked at Williams and said, "Can you get someone from forensics to dust the drawer ASAP?"

Williams nodded and went out.

"Maybe we can catch a gun thief," Deacon said.

*

Chapter 24

"The person was smart enough not to leave his prints on the gun, I would think he wouldn't leave prints on the drawer," Warren said.

"You're not helping your case. Have a little faith in forensics. There were two drawers involved, a search to find the key and the key. One of those had to have a tell-tale print. We'll wait and see," Deacon said.

In observation, Dave's cell phone rang, he answered, "Hello, Dave Chandler here." He listened for a minute, talked briefly, then hung up. "That was my friend Warren Stevens from the FBI. You've met him. He's coming in early on an FBI charter jet. He's bringing Virgil. They are going to be landing at McCarran Airport commercial terminals in an hour. Hanger 452. Can we get there from here?"

"You got it." Jim stood and went out the door to the room with the men. He quietly opened the door and signaled Deacon.

Deacon excused himself and went out to Jim. "What's up?"

"Dave's FBI friend Warren Stevens is arriving at McCarran in an hour. I'm taking Dave there to pick them up."

"Go, we can help Greg here. We need forensics to get back on everything involved in this case. So go take care of business."

"I'll check in later. Thanks," Jim said and turned to Dave. The men left and went out to Jim's Crown Vic. He drove over to the airport and around to the commercial terminals. They drove around to the hangar in question and parked.

"You've known Stevens for a while?"

"We've been friends since way back," Dave said. "He's always been there to help with the serial killers and terrorist we had to deal with. Good man to have on our side."

"I remember he was a whirlwind when we had to find and save Penny and Sarah from the drug people."

"I'd trust him with my life. And I have."

They sat watching jets land and pull onto the tarmac by the hangars. Finally one landed and pulled up to the hangar they were waiting at. Jim and Dave exited the car and went to the jet as it parked. The ramp came down and out bounced Special Agent Warren Stevens. Dave's deputy, Virgil, staggered down the stairs from the jet, looking ill.

Dave and Jim laughed when Virgil sat down on the tarmac and patted the ground. Dave went to Stevens and they hugged a man hug.

"Virgil hasn't been the best passenger," Stevens said. "He spent most of the flight in the head."

"Good thing you can make it without losing your cookies," Jim laughed.

"Well, I wasn't going to hold his head out of the toilet. I just hoped that the pressure didn't suck him out the hole." Stevens looked at Jim coming over. "Hey, Jim, how's that sexy wife of yours?"

"Still sexy. How are you?"

"Good. Now I need to hear about this banned chemical coming here to poison people."

"Let's get you and Virgil to your hotel rooms and then we can sit down and go over details," Jim said.

"I hope it's better than one of those sleazy Strip motels," Stevens said with a smile.

Jim pointed to the huge pyramid across from the airport. "Penny set you up in the Luxor Hotel, so is that good enough?"

Stevens grinned at Dave and said, "Luxor? Jim's wife has taste, but why is she married to Jim?"

"Hey, I'm right here. Penny and I get along fine," Jim protested.

"Don't panic, Jimbo. I'm just pulling your chain," Stevens said.

Jim looked at Dave and asked, "How do you put up with him?"

"It's not easy, I have to slap him around occasionally to keep him in line," Dave responded with a laugh.

"Okay, let's pick Virgil up off the pavement and go to our hotel rooms," Dave said. They went to Virgil and helped him up, then they went to Jim's car after taking the baggage from the jet and put it in the trunk of the car.

A half hour later, they were registering at the hotel, making changes in the reservations for early arrival. Jim called Penny and told her of the changes. She said to say hi to the men.

They went up to the room and Dave took Virgil aside and asked, "Is Mike watching the office?"

"Yep, they sent in a deputy from Olympia to help watch the county while I'm gone. They have it under control."

The men spent a little time unpacking and changing clothes more suited to the weather in Las Vegas. Dave and Jim sat in the living area of the room when there was a knocking at the door. Dave stood and went to open the door. It was Sarah and Penny.

Sarah flew in and went straight to Warren Stevens. "Warren, so good to see you," she said as she gave the man a big hug.

"Hey, unhand my wife," Dave joked.

They continued to hug as Stevens said, "Suck it up, country boy. She's mine now."

Sarah pushed back and hit Stevens on the shoulder. "Don't get ahead of yourself. You haven't earned the right to take me over." She went over by Penny on the couch.

"So, fill me in on the details of your case," Stevens asked and sat on the easy chair. Dave and Jim pulled chairs over and sat.

Jim started. "Going to the beginning, we had a case of a woman poisoned by sunblock laced with Tetraethyl Lead."

"I've heard of the stuff. It's deadly and getting it on a person's body can cause death," Warren said.

Jim continued with the story of Sam's female employee dying from exposure to the sunblock and through to the death of Hallson in his motel room.

"We think the poisoning will stop now that Hallson is out of the picture. Unless there were others involved. Now we have to get Greg Warren off of murder charges for Hallson's death," Jim said.

"I remember Greg from when I was here last, nice guy. I'll give you any help the bureau can supply on this. I already informed my section chief about the little details I knew. Since the banned chemicals were transported across state line, we can step in. But I think I'll hold off since you seem to have the situation in hand so far."

"This is now a murder case. The poisonings are attributed to our murdered victim. Hopefully with his death the poisonings will stop," Jim said.

"Do you have any other suspects in the murder other than Greg?"

"We're looking at a lieutenant of the homicide squad that took a position that Greg was hoping to get. We think he may be wanting to prevent Greg from ever getting the job."

"Up in Seattle, the poisonings were getting heavy notice on our news channels. This is becoming a high profile case now. Maybe this lieutenant wanted the glory for himself and is trying to get Greg disgraced and out of the picture."

"Good point. Deacon is having Greg's desk dusted for prints to see who may have taken his extra backup piece and used it to kill Hallson. It had to be someone in the squad, Greg would never do it."

"Would your captain mind if I came in and talked to a few people? Maybe the presence of the FBI would shake up the actual suspect."

"Sounds like a good idea," Jim said and looked to Penny. "You wouldn't be upset if we left you two to your own devices?"

"Of course not. We expect our husbands to fight crime more than pay attention to us," Penny said.

"Good, that's the attitude. Okay men, shall we go fight crime," Jim said with a smirk.

Penny stood and whacked Jim on the arm. She waved to Sarah to follow. "We are going to do what we do best, shop and spend your money." She gave a sinister laugh and the two of them left.

"Women can be evil. That's why I never married," Stevens said.

Dave laughed and said, "You never married because no woman would have you."

Stevens replied, "At least I'm happy and have all my own money, shall we go?"

*

Chapter 25

Virgil said he wanted to go explore Vegas. Dave warned him not to get in any trouble. He left and Jim took Dave and Stevens to his car.

The three men drove to the LVPD precinct and went in. Deacon and Lynn were in the squad room talking to Detective Williams. Deacon smiled when the men came up.

"Special Agent Stevens, good to see you again. Are you here to help us?" Deacon said.

"Hey, DeAngelo, good to see you again. I'm always ready to help. Are you still working here?"

"No, I retired and I'm working for Jim now. Better conditions, better boss," Deacon replied.

"Ah, you know how to butter me up," Jim laughed.

"Lynn, are you still married to this big lug?" Stevens asked her.

"Yes, and we're parents now," she replied. "Baby girl."

"Congratulations. So how's the poisoning case progressing?"

"Are you here in an official capacity?" Williams asked.

"My boss at the bureau knows about the poisonings and I was asked to investigate the use of the chemical since I was coming here for the wedding. So I guess I'm official. Now talk to me," Stevens said.

"I'm sure Jim filled you in on the details. We're at a point now of trying to get Greg Warren off on suspicion of murder charges," Lynn said.

"He hasn't been formally charged?"

"Not yet, we don't have much to go on other than the evidence of gun ownership and ballistics. Captain Weber is stalling on charging Greg," Williams said.

"Jim did fill me in on the details. There haven't been any more poisonings?"

"None. But we put out the info to the media and they've been warning people about the use of any type of body creams. We had a number of people bringing in lotions that they say didn't smell right. About ten percent of those were tainted. Probably left over from the first batch that went out to the public."

Jim was looking around the squad room and noticed that Boering was standing off the side in his office watching the men. He saw Jim looking at him, so he turned and went to where Jim couldn't see him. Jim still didn't like the man.

"May I talk to Greg?" Stevens asked.

"Sure, come with me," Williams said. Everyone followed Williams to the room where Greg Warren was still sitting. He smiled when he saw Agent Stevens enter. Everyone else went to observations.

"Agent Stevens, are you here to save me?"

"Greg, if I can I will. Now tell me everything you did involving this Hallson character."

Greg Warren went over the details of his involvement before and after the murder of Hallson. Stevens sat listening as everyone else waited in observation, watching Stevens talking to Greg.

"I never saw or met Hallson at all until he was dead in the motel room," Greg said.

"Do you always leave your extra backup gun in your drawer?"

"I lock it in my desk, yes."

"Did anyone else know it was there?"

"A few people. But anyone who watched me could see it was there when I would switch off my backup piece. I need to have a change of guns, I sweat a lot and I have to clean the weapon regularly."

"So others knew the gun was there?"

Greg paused and thought. "Yeah, I guess it wasn't much of a secret."

"Did Lieutenant Boering know it was there?"

"I couldn't say, it's possible."

"What does he have against you?"

Greg paused again, thinking. "I was expecting to take Deacon's position as Lieutenant of the squad when he left. I already passed the exams and was on the list. But the brass brought in Boering. Weber told me he wasn't happy about it, but he couldn't buck the system."

"So, you were pushed back in favor of Boering?"

"Yeah, I guess you could say that. I wasn't happy, but I accepted it."

"Has he said anything to you about his taking the position?"

Greg paused again. He looked uncomfortable, then said, "He threatened me the other day about me trying to take his job. He said, 'If you think you're going to get my job, think twice' and I left it at that. I didn't think much of his threat, but now that my reputation is on the line, it worries me."

Stevens turned to the mirror and said, "Why don't you guys come in here."

Everyone went around to interrogations and waited for Stevens to talk.

"As I see it, which I'm sure we all do, if we assume Greg is innocent then someone in this squad was stupid enough to take Greg's gun and kill the suspect." Everyone nodded in agreement. "So this person took the gun and had to have known where Hallson was in order to kill him."

"So you think the person in the squad knew about the poisoning plot also? Maybe from the start?" Deacon asked.

"It makes sense. If this person knew where Hallson was, he could have easily captured him and been a hero. But if he brought Hallson in alive, it may have turned out that he was involved with the poisonings."

"So he murders Hallson to cover his involvement, and places the murder on Greg," Jim said.

"That's my feeling on it. You have a real dirty cop in this squad."

"Boering," Lynn said, "I never liked that man."

"But how do we prove it without making waves in the department?" Greg asked.

"What do you know about Boering?" Stevens asked.

"He's a dickhead," Lynn said. Everyone laughed.

"Okay, that's a start. What kind of cop is he?"

"He's pushy, arrogant, doesn't play well with others and he's secretive," Greg said. "I worked with him once before on a case that we shared with North Vegas PD. He didn't like us being in on the bust. I'm sure he wanted it all to himself, to get his closing rates up. Looks good on his record."

"So this poisoning case comes up and he doesn't get in on it?" Stevens asked.

"Actually, he didn't really seem interested in it. He never moved on it and I got assigned to it."

"So maybe he was hoping you'd take lead on it? Getting you in position to take a fall."

"He went to a lot of extremes to set it up, murdering people other than Hallson. Just to frame Greg," Jim said.

"Maybe he had his eye on solving the case and taking the glory. But Greg got there first, so his plan was falling apart. Both of the poisoners are now dead. The chemical barrels are missing and all is quiet now other than Greg being involved in Hallson's murder."

"Weber said that Boering believed Greg was guilty. I don't know what he based that on," Williams said.

"Maybe we should ask him," Stevens said.

"Want me to see if he'll join us?" Williams asked.

"No, let's go out to his office and talk to him there." Stevens stood and said to Greg, "Hang in here, I'll see what I can find out." He left the room followed by the others as Greg sat looking dejected.

"Maybe we shouldn't all attack him at the same time." Stevens said to his companions. "Might make him uncooperative. Williams can take me to him and I'll see what he has to say."

Deacon, Lynn, Jim and Dave said they would wait in the squad room. Williams took Stevens to Boering's office where they found him sitting at his desk going over some papers.

"Lieutenant, someone here to talk to you," Williams said and pointed to Stevens. The agent went into Boering's office and up to his desk.

"I'm Special Agent Warren Stevens, FBI from out of Seattle," he said showing his badge. "I was assigned to investigate movement of a banned chemical that came from our state to Las Vegas. I'm sure you know all the details."

Boering gave Stevens a hard stare and finally said, "A little out of your jurisdiction, Agent Stevens."

"Oh no, Lieutenant. You should know that the FBI has jurisdiction anywhere in the contiguous United States. Including Las Vegas. I need to talk to you about the poisonings and the subsequent murder of two of the criminals involved."

"We know how one of the criminals died. Greg Warren murdered him," Boering said bluntly.

"You know that for a fact? What advantage would killing Hallson have? Detective Warren could easily have brought him in and closed part of the case. Maybe Hallson would have given the names of the others involved in the poisonings. You think that would be possible?"

"A little late to dwell on that. We won't know now that the two men involved are dead."

"Yes, very convenient. Tell me something, why would Detective Warren take his extra backup weapon, go find and shoot Hallson, then leave his gun to be found at the crime scene?"

"Maybe because he's stupid. How should I know? It's his gun that killed Hallson and he has no alibi for where he was during the murder. That's good enough for me."

"Ah, just close the case and put Warren on trial for murder. You'd like that, wouldn't you? Get rid of the only other detective who could take your job. Nice and tied up for you."

Boering stood forcefully shoving his chair back and said, "If you are insinuating that I had anything to do with this, you're blowing smoke."

"Fine, we'll see what comes out when the smoke clears," Stevens said quietly and left the room followed by Williams.

*

Chapter 26

Williams was grinning widely and holding in a laugh as the two men went back to the group standing in the hall by the break room.

"That should stir his blood," Stevens said. "I'm going out on a limb to say he's involved in this up to his moustache. It's a bad moustache too."

They heard a voice coming towards them, it was Weber. "Do we have a party going on?" he asked.

"No, Captain. This is Special Agent Warren Stevens from the FBI. He's here to help on the poisoning case since the poison came from his area," Jim said.

"Good to meet you, Stevens. The poisonings seem to have let up, what with the deaths of the men involved. Do you have any theories?"

"Not yet, Captain. I just got into town and everyone has been updating me. Is Detective Warren going to be charged?"

"Frankly I don't believe he did it, but the chain of evidence is there, flimsy as it is. I'm letting him go pending further investigation. Have you talked to him?"

"I have and I agree, he wouldn't have committed this murder, the facts are not all there."

"Well, maybe with all these investigators," he said, pointing to everyone there, "you can find out just who did commit the murder."

"We'll do our best," Stevens replied.

"Very good, carry on. I've work to do." Weber smiled to everyone and went off.

"Odd little man," Stevens said.

"You got that right," Jim replied. "Now what do we do to prove Boering is behind this?"

Stevens looked at Williams, "Since you're local police, you can get me into the crime scene at the motel, right?"

"Sure," Williams replied.

"The rest of you sit around the squad room and hopefully Boering will get curious. If he asks where Williams or I am, tell him. He may wonder why we're going there. Let's keep him wondering, he'll eventually slip up."

Everyone agreed and went to Williams' desk and milled around. Stevens left with Williams and then Greg Warren came out from the hallway of interrogation. Deacon and Jim went over to greet him and brought him back to his desk.

"I can't do anything," Greg said. "I'm on suspension pending the outcome of the murder investigation. Where's Williams?"

"He and Stevens went to the motel to take a look around. Not that they'll find anything but we're trying to spook Boering," Jim said.

"Speaking of Boering, where is he?"

"Last we saw, he was in his office," Deacon said as Lynn and Dave came over.

As they stood there Boering came out of his office. "What are you doing at your desk, Warren? You're on suspension. And why are you still here, Deacon?"

"In case you haven't heard, Weber assigned us as consultants to LVPD, and we are consulting. Williams and Agent Stevens went back to the motel to investigate."

"What the hell are they expecting to find there?" Boering was looking worried.

"Who knows? Agent Stevens is a crack investigator for the FBI, if anyone can find clues, it will be him," Jim said.

"Fine," Boering said tersely and went back to his office.

"That man seems concerned," Dave said.

"You got that. Now that Boering knows they are at the motel, shall we get out of here and go get some food?" Jim said.

"You always think of food during a crisis, don't you?" Lynn said.

"Got to feed the brain cells so we can solve this thing. How about pizza?"

Everyone agreed and they went out to their cars and drove to Angelo's.

"What do you expect to find?" Williams asked Stevens as they moved around the motel room.

"Haven't the foggiest idea. But something may pop up," Stevens replied. He looked at the door and asked, "This wasn't forced?"

"No, CSI said the door wasn't forced. They say the killer had to have been known by the vic to have let him in."

"No signs of defensive wounds on the vic?"

"He didn't fight the perp. I think he let the man in and then was shot right away. His body was close to the door, so they didn't move in very far."

"How many shots?"

"Three, two to the chest and one to the head. Shot through a pillow to muffle the sound."

"Yes, the final kill shot to the head. Had to be a pro, or a cop." Stevens was pulling drawers and looking through them. "Not many clothes at all. The vic hadn't planned on staying long."

"Desk clerk said he only paid for two nights. He was supposed to be out this morning."

"Did he call for a cab to be here? If he was taking a plane flight he'd have to be there on time."

"I didn't think to check the airlines. I'll call Electronics and see if they can get his name on any flights."

"Good. That may explain why he was murdered also. Prevent him from running."

"But why a plane?"

"I was told he torched his truck so he had no transportation. A quick ride to the airport by cab and he'd be on his way out of town."

"True, I'll make the call and see what can be found." He turned and went out the door to the walkway to make his call.

Stevens wandered around the room, nosing into every place he could get his nose in. The bathroom had very few articles that would show the man was settling in the room. He waited for Williams to come back in.

"They're getting the manifest for planes heading out today. We also have his credit card so they're cross-checking to see what he purchased. This all happened in the last 24 hours, so we are still touching base on the evidence."

"Did they check the phone logs from this room?"

"A couple calls, mostly to our precinct. Which is why they are assuming Warren was in on the whole thing."

"Or calling Boering."

"Everyone is working on this, we want to prove Greg is innocent."

"Fresh cases need to be solved fast. Evidence goes bad if left too long. Twenty-four to forty-eight hours, before the trail dries up. Nothing more I see here, hopefully Boering got nosy enough to inquire as to where we were. Let's go back."

They closed up the motel room and drove back to the precinct. They found everyone was gone.

"That's nice, desert us." Stevens pulled out his phone and called Dave. "Where are you guys?" he asked when Dave answered. He listened for a minute than asked Williams, "Do you know a place called Mama Mia?" Williams said he did and Stevens said, "Don't eat all the pizza, we'll be right there."

Jim was disappointed that Angelo wasn't in today. He wanted to introduce him to Dave and Stevens. They'd have to come back another time.

"So where are we going to have the bachelor party?" Stevens asked.

"I was thinking right here," Jim said. "There's a back room where we can play poker and swill beer until we turn blue."

"No strippers?" Stevens asked.

"Not if you want to live. My wife and Sarah aren't allowing us the pleasure of strippers."

"Strange, Penny said something about going to see the 'Thunder from Down Under' male strip show for Sarah's bachelorette party," Lynn said. "Oops, maybe I shouldn't have said that."

"Or you said it deliberately. Thanks for the heads up," Jim said with a grin.

*

Chapter 27

Penny and Sarah stood on the concourse waiting for Lois to disembark from her plane. She came in early since everyone else was in town and she didn't want to miss a thing. Sarah had called Virgil at the hotel to go with them to get Lois and help with baggage. He stood watching for the woman as the passengers exited the plane.

"Sarah, yoo hoo!" came a familiar voice from the crowd. "Here I am, Sarah!" Lois yelled over the heads of the other passengers. She came bounding out of the crowd and over to Penny and Sarah. She saw Virgil and said, "Virgil, be a dear and get my baggage."

Virgil grinned and went off as the women were hugging and making little squeals. They all walked to the concourse baggage pickup and watched Virgil standing at the luggage carousel watching everyone's luggage roll around. Lois yelled that they were matching blue Samsonites, which Virgil had no idea what that meant.

"So, it is hot here," Lois said.

"You're in the air conditioned building, Lois. You haven't even been outside yet," Penny said.

"Oh, well, I feel warm."

"That heavy coat you're wearing doesn't help," Sarah said and helped her out of the coat.

"It was a little chilly when I left the Seattle airport. What's the temperature here?"

"It's about one-hundred and three degrees outside," Penny said. "But we won't be out in it very long. Besides it's very dry here, not like Seattle. You'll hardly notice the heat once you've been in it a while."

"Oh, my. That is hot. Well, I'll have to put up with it I suppose," Lois said.

"We spend more time in air conditioning than we do outside. So don't worry," Penny said with a grin.

"I want to see the Strip and visit the Elvis museum," Lois said excitedly.

Penny crinkled her nose hearing the name Elvis. She was not going to take this woman to see Elvis. She would have Jim take her.

"We'll work it out," Penny said. "Besides you have four beautiful days to see the sights. We go out mostly at night when it's cooler. We'll take you to see the Strip, and I hope you have comfortable walking shoes. It's about a mile journey up and down the Strip."

"Oh, my. Yes, I do have my walking shoes packed." She saw her luggage coming down the row and yelled, "Virgil, there they are. The two blue ones." She pointed and Virgil grabbed them as they rolled by. "Good, that's all I have now. Where are we staying?"

"I've booked you a room at the Luxor Hotel, it's the big pyramid building with all the Egyptian décor."

"I've seen that on TV, I love it, shall we go?" Lois was on her way out, even though she had no idea where she was going.

"We'll have to keep an eye on her, she tends to bull her way through life," Sarah told Penny.

Penny grabbed Lois' arm and said, "This way, Lois. Just follow me."

Virgil brought up the rear with the bags.

~~*~~

In the dining room at Angelo's restaurant everyone had finished their meals and sat talking.

"So how do we draw Boering out? He's not real bright from what I've seen so far," Sevens said.

"I have a thought," Jim said. "The barrels of lead have to be somewhere. I'm sure Boering knows where they are. If we can make him think that we got a tip on their location, we could follow him when he goes to see if they are still there."

"Wow, you thought that up all by yourself?" Deacon mocked.

"You said before that I was your boss, so I can fire you. Keep that in mind."

"Actually, it's a good idea," Stevens said. "If he thinks we are on the trail of the lead, he'd have to do something about it. I have a feeling his prints are all over the barrels and he wouldn't want them found."

"What if he buried them out in the desert?" Lynn asked.

"Doesn't matter. If he thinks we suspect where they are, he'll do what he can to make sure they don't point to him."

"Fine, how do we get this plan started?" Dave asked.

"We can fake a call to the precinct and ask to speak to a detective to give him the info on where the barrels are. That detective would have to be Williams, since he's heading this case now. We have to time this just right, so we don't have to say where we were told to find the barrels, just let Boering know we are going to get them."

"We would need two teams, one to go after the fake location and one to follow Boering," Deacon said. "Jim can go with Williams, Dave and Stevens, and Lynn, Greg, and I can follow Boering. We'll be waiting outside by his car and hopefully he'll take the bait."

"That works for me," Stevens said. Everyone agreed. Jim paid the bill for the food and they all went to their cars and drove back to the precinct.

In the parking lot, Deacon, Greg and Lynn stayed at Deacon's car as the others went inside. Boering was in his office as they slipped over to Williams' desk.

Jim set up the scam. "Williams will stay at this desk and take the pretend call from the anonymous source. Dave and Stevens will go with me over by Boering's office. Williams when you finish your fake call, you'll yell to us loudly so Boering can hear, that you have a location on where the lead barrels are at. Then you rush like hell out so Boering can't stop you to ask any questions. We'll follow you and hope he takes the bait."

"Sounds good," Stevens said. "Shall we take a stroll?"

Jim, Dave and Stevens walked past Boering's office and slowed down. Boering was eyeing them. Jim was carefully watching Williams as he put the phone back down. The room was so noisy that Boering couldn't hear a phone ring or not.

Williams stood and yelled, "Jim, just got a call about where we can find the missing barrels of lead. Let's get there quickly." Then he rushed out of the squad room. Jim watched Boering as he heard what was said. He had a surprised look on his face.

"Let's get moving before he stops us," Jim said and they rushed away. On the way out Jim said to his companions, "I think he heard everything, so I'll call Deacon and tell them to be ready." They rushed out to the parking lot and over to Williams' unmarked car. They got in and drove out. Jim had called Deacon to say Boering may have taken the bait so watch for him.

"Where are we going?" Williams asked Jim.

"I don't know. Just park across the street and watch for Boering."

Williams pulled into the parking lot of an office building and turned to face the road. They could see where Boering's car was parked, but they couldn't see Deacon. He had to be around the side of the building. About three minutes later, Boering rushed to his car and drove out. He was followed by Deacon at a good distance.

"This car is dark enough and unmarked, so Boering wouldn't know we were following also. So keep behind Deacon." Jim got on his phone and called Lynn. She came on.

"We've got him in sight. He's heading north," she said.

"I know, we're right behind you."

Jim could see Lynn look back, as did Warren. He waved. "Keep on his tail. I'm sure he's going to where the barrels are to see if we have the right location. Then we got him."

Dave was in the back seat with Stevens and said, "I love it when a plan comes together." They all laughed.

Boering drove out Flamingo Road and turned north on Rainbow. He drove on until he got to West Spring Mountain Drive and turned west. This area was all dug up for what probably would be a subdivision or a casino. There were scattered work buildings and a number of cargo trucks parked in the dirt.

"Nice place to hide his barrels," Jim said as they slowed. Boering pulled into a drive going out to the work buildings. He stopped but didn't get out of his car.

"We have to catch him with the barrels, or the bust is no good," Williams said.

"He's waiting to see if anyone is showing. Let's just sit here a bit. Jim called Lynn again. "Hang out here until he does something, we need to catch him with the barrels." Lynn agreed and they sat waiting.

"About ten minutes later, Boering finally got out of his car and walked to a small shed. They could see him opening the lock on the door and going in. "We have to move now," Jim said on the phone and to Williams.

The two cars roared into the dusty lot and up to the shed. Everyone jumped from their cars and rushed the shed. As they were getting there a gunshot rang out and everyone scattered.

"Boering, you can't get away now, give up," Greg Warren yelled from behind a pile of lumber.

"Screw you, Warren!" came a voice and another gunshot.

Jim saw Stevens creep low around the shed and stopped just before the door. Another gunshot rang out and then it was quiet.

Stevens dove in front of the door to the ground and held his gun out. He lay there a moment until he stood and went in the shed. Everyone ran to the door and found Stevens standing over the body of Boering. He had blood streaming from his head, self-inflicted, Stevens said.

"Why would he kill himself?" Greg asked. "We didn't have that much on him, he could have bluffed his way out."

Stevens was looking at a couple sheets of paper from an envelope he found on top of one barrel. "He was up to his ears in this. These papers are confessions from Hallson about the whole plot. As I read it, Boering set this up to make himself look good. Hallson said he didn't know the lead would kill people, just make them sick. I guess he wasn't very bright. Boering knew him from a prior bust and recruited him to help with this plot. I guess Hallson didn't figure Boering would kill him."

Jim looked at Greg Warren and said, "Well, that lets you off."

*

Chapter 28

Weber came out to the site personally to take a look at the situation. A command officer had taken his own life and he wanted answers. He stood reading the confession, left by Hallson, now in a plastic sleeve. Fingerprints would need to be taken from the paper.

"Warren, you are reinstated," Weber said to Greg. "Let's clean this affair up and file it all away. This is a sticky mess that we had a crooked cop. I want this kept under wraps if at all possible. I'll make a statement to the media that we caught the two men who were poisoning lotions. This is the end to this case. Good job, men," he said to everyone standing around.

"Now I can tell Trapper and Sam we got the killers. Shame we couldn't capture Boering alive," Jim said.

"Boering knew if he went to prison, he'd be dead in days. He put a whole lot of men away who would love to get their hands on him," Warren said.

"Whatever, it's over and I have a bachelor party to concentrate on now," Jim said. He turned to Dave and Stevens and said, "Let's blow this pop stand. Deacon, can you give us a ride out of here?"

"I'm part of the party, right?" Deacon asked.

"Of course. Only if we get moving."

They went to the car and Lynn said, "I need to find Penny and Sarah. I'll call them and you can drop me wherever they are."

She made the call and said to Deacon that they were at the Luxor. They drove out from the construction site and over to the Luxor. They dropped Lynn off and she kissed Deacon goodbye. The men drove over to the precinct where Jim picked up his car, then they drove back to their office and parked in the back.

Jim led them to the break room and told them to relax, then he went up front.

Lacey was at her desk and Jim asked, "Where's Trapper?"

"He took Sam out for dinner. Earl is following a cheating spouse and Buck is still on vacation back in Michigan."

"I forgot about Buck. It's been so quiet around here without him. We'll be in the break room relaxing."

"Did you solve the sunblock killings?"

"Yes, we did. It's all over now. That's all I can say."

"Oh, being secretive now?"

"Always. It's my curse. Hold my calls."

"You really want me to say it?"

"Yes, I miss your sarcasm."

"Okay…No one ever calls you."

"Thank you Lacey, now go tell Tracey that you two can go home. Lock the doors."

Lacey didn't wait, she grabbed her purse and went to the front lobby to tell Tracey to leave. They did and Jim smiled.

~~*~~

Lynn was sitting in the spacious living area of the hotel room where they put Lois. The older woman was changing into more comfortable clothes. She now had on Capri pants, sandals, a straw hat with wide brim and a bright orange top. She looked more like she should be in Jamaica, rather than Las Vegas.

"Lois, you are a sight. You'll stand out in the crowds of Vegas," Penny said.

"At least we won't lose her," Sarah laughed.

"So are we going to explore the Strip?" Lois asked.

"If we walk from here and head north we can cover the west side of the Strip. Up to the Old Sahara and then back down," Penny explained. "There's a gift shop I'm sure you will love. It's considered the largest gift shop in the world and no one has ever challenged it."

"When do we go to see the Elvis museum?" Lois asked.

Penny looked at Lynn and said, "You can take Sarah and Lois to the Elvis museum. I have a feeling I'm not going to be feeling well then."

Lynn smiled and said she would.

"So how did your sunblock case turn out?" Penny asked. "Did the men do a good job or did you have to help them?"

"Of course, I have to say I was an integral part of the case. I had to be there to help Greg get off murder charges." Lynn said.

"So he's good now?"

"Yes, he's back on the force and Las Vegas is safe to slather up with sunblock."

"Speaking of sunblock, will I need some?" Lois asked.

"All the sunblock products in Vegas have been recalled. They were too strong," Lynn said.

"Well, I have my floppy straw hat to protect me."

"Let's go, girls. The Strip awaits," Penny said.

They left the room and down to the street. They walked past the Mandalay Bay Hotel just south of the Luxor and then turned back up past the Luxor to the Excalibur Hotel/Casino. Penny took them through the big castle building and then back out. They saw New York, New York as Penny gave details about Jim working in the casino mall at a magic shop.

They made it up to the Bellagio and stood watching the ballet of the fountain streams of dancing water. An hour later they made it up to the gift shop. By now Lois was starting to wear down, but seeing the gift shop revitalized her. She just about danced through the building.

They finally caught a cab and took it back to the hotel, Lois carrying her bags of souvenirs. "I didn't realize how big Vegas really was," Lois admitted.

"Yes, you have to be in good shape to see it all in one day," Penny said. "We have tomorrow to explore further."

At the hotel, Sarah told Lois that she should get some rest tonight, they could start again tomorrow.

"Yes, dear, I am tired. I'll get some sleep and you come by to get me," Lois said at her door. They let her go in and then went back down stairs.

"Okay, where's a wild dance club?" Sarah said.

"It will be coming when we go out soon. For now, we need to rest." They went to Penny's car and drove back to Penny's house after they dropped Lynn off. Dave and Jim were back at the house, after dropping Warren Stevens off at his hotel.

"We decided to write this day off. We had a busy day. We can regroup tomorrow," Jim said as Penny come up to him sitting by the pool in the loungers.

"Aren't you two going to swim?" Sarah asked.

"Oh, Jim doesn't like the water. It's a rare occasion that he gets in. But that doesn't stop us. Shall we change?" Penny asked and led Sarah in to get their swimsuits on.

"If we can't get strippers, at least we can watch our wives in bikinis." Jim said.

"I'm all for that," Dave smiled.

*

Chapter 29

Two days later and about fifty miles of walking the Strip for Lois and Sarah, then one trip to the Elvis Museum, Sarah was anxious to get married. Her wedding gown was fitted and ready. The floral arrangements were made and a minister was found by Lynn to suit Penny and Sarah. He was a non-denominational minister named Reverend John Gross and he said he was available to preside over the wedding.

On the bride's side of the wedding party were Penny, Lynn, Lois, Lacey and Tracey. Sarah wished her longtime friend Connie could have made it from New York, but it was not possible.

On the groom's side were Warren Stevens, Jim, Virgil, Deacon and Trapper. Earl came in for the wedding but wasn't one of the groomsmen. Jim had talked to Buck out in Michigan and he regretted not being able to be there. A family emergency prevented him from leaving.

The wedding day arrived and it was beautiful in Vegas. Not too hot and yet still sunny as always.

They opted to have the wedding at the Bellagio, outside by the fountain, so Jim pulled some strings with a few people he knew and arranged for it. Penny talked her talk show producer into filming the whole thing, so Sarah and Dave would have a memory video.

Greg Warren had a number of police officers arranged to keep curiosity seekers away from the wedding. Captain Weber was invited and he said he'd show up.

Up in the hotel room occupied by Stevens, the men sat waiting to drive over to the Bellagio. "This was a lot easier the last time Sarah and I got married here. Simple in and out," Dave said.

"I told you Penny would make a production out of it," Jim replied with a laugh.

"Well, Sarah is happy and that's all that counts."

Stevens came out from the bedroom dressed in his tux, looking debonair. "I could get used to this outfit. I look like a foreign spy."

"You look like a maître d' at a restaurant," Dave said.

"I'm an elegant maître d' then."

Jim's phone buzzed and he answered, it was Penny. "What's up?" He listened and then hung up.

"Seems the bride is getting impatient and the bridal party is ready to go. So let's head to the car and go."

"They drove the couple blocks to the Bellagio and into valet parking. They exited the car and walked around to the front where the wedding was to take place. Warren was at the perimeter where they strung yellow tape to keep intruders back. Jim laughed at the sight of the tape.

"Your wedding is now a crime scene," Jim said to Dave.

"I always knew that, my quick death."

Jim looked at Trapper and said, "Will, remember when you and Becker poured red dye in the fountain?"

"I wouldn't say that too loud, the hotel wasn't happy about it. They never knew who did it," Trapper said quietly.

Shelby Francis, the wedding planner was still arranging the flowers and setting things up. Jim knew they were going to Angelo's for the reception. Angelo said he'd fix the banquet room up real nice. Jim loaned out his mini-limo for the bride and groom being driven by Fred to drive around the city. Fred fixed the limo up with signs and flowers. Jim was pleased with everything.

The men went up to the flowered arch at the head of the patio at the Bellagio fountain, where they met Reverend Gross. He greeted them and commented on how this was his first wedding in such impressive surroundings.

"It's the least we could do for our friends," Jim said and they lined up for the procession.

Shelby signaled the person handling the music and out blared the Wedding March. Shelby ran around to the door leading into the building where the women waited. She signaled them to come out.

They walked down the steps and over toward the flowered arch. Jim could hear Dave say, "Wow, she's beautiful" when he saw Sarah.

The women joined up at the makeshift altar and Reverend Gross started.

"Dearly beloved, we are gathered here to join David Chandler with Sarah Chandler, once again." He smiled and continued. He asked if anyone knew why these two shouldn't be joined, and no one said a word. Jim had told Warren to shoot anyone speaking out.

The Reverend said a few things about love and marriage, then had Dave and Sarah read the vows they wrote. Dave did fine, but Sarah choked briefly, then carried on.

They exchanged rings, the same ones they had when they first got married. Dave had mentioned buying new rings but Sarah insisted on the ones they took their vows with the first time.

Reverend Gross pronounced them husband and wife, again. Everyone laughed and cheered.

Jim had arranged for the Bellagio to set off the big dance number of the fountain water stream and everyone watched. Then Jim called Fred to say to bring the car around to the side to pick up Dave and Sarah. He said he was already there.

The newlyweds came down from the patio altar as everyone threw birdseed, at Penny's insistence. She was thinking about the birds.

Dave thanked Jim and Penny and took Sarah to the car for a ride around Vegas. Warren had arranged for a patrol car to lead them with flashers and sirens. They drove off as Penny stood next to Jim.

"Shall we ask the Reverend to give us a quick renewal of our vows?" she asked him.

Jim looked back and the minister was gone. "Too late, he said he had another wedding to go to."

"Well, then, we will do it on our tenth anniversary."

"Works for me," Jim said and took Penny to the valet parking to get his car. Trapper found Sam in the small crowd of people Jim and Penny invited and said he was going with Sam. Jim told Stevens, Virgil and Lois they could ride with them to the reception. They got the car and drove over to Mama Mia Restaurant. Angelo greeted them at the door and escorted them to the banquet room.

As soon as they walked in, Jim was overtaken by what Angelo had done to decorate the room. Streamers and flowers everywhere. And a big banner congratulating the bride and groom.

"Angelo, there's a big tip in this for you," he said to his friend.

"Aw, Mr. R. it was my pleasure. Glad to do this for your friends."

"Well, you are my big friend, Angelo. Don't ever forget that."

Angelo excused himself to go get the food ready. About a half hour and a couple beers later, Jim was happily seated next to his wife. The bride and groom were still out riding around.

"You never did say how your bachelor party went last night," Penny asked.

"Nope and I'm not telling."

"There weren't any strippers, were there?" Penny poked Jim in his ribs.

"As much as Trapper wanted to bring some, there were none. We just played poker and relaxed, that's all." Jim kissed Penny on her cheek and said, "Dave was already married to Sarah so it was just a night out with the boys."

"Good for you," Penny said.

"How was your bachelorette party?"

"Tame. We went to see 'Thunder from Down Under,' but they didn't have a show last night. We were disappointed but we went to see the Blue Man Group. It was a great show."

"So were you happy with all this?"

"Very. I wish I could do this more often."

"Maybe Shelby has an opening for a wedding planner. You could make a full time job out of it."

Penny looked at Jim and grinned, "Hmm."

*

Chapter 30

Ten minutes later, Jim wondered where the bride and groom were, so he called Fred. Fred answered and said, "We're just outside the restaurant. Seems Dave and Sarah are more interested in making out in the limo than going in."

Jim laughed out loud and told Penny what Fred said. Penny yelled, "Tell those two to get in here. They have guests who are waiting."

Fred said he heard her and would relay the message. About ten minutes later the newlyweds came in. Everyone cheered and made noises. Warren Stevens went to Dave and said something, then led them to the head table where they were seated. Stevens had been selected to be the best man over Jim and Virgil, since he knew Dave longer than anyone. He called attention to the guests of about fifty people whom Jim and Penny invited.

There were a number of friends and acquaintances from both Penny's studio and the police. Most of the police had shared in the chase to find Penny and Sarah when they were taken by the drug cartel. So they knew the bride and groom. Even Captain Weber showed up.

Stevens made his speech. "I want to say I don't understand why Sarah would remarry Dave. As a lowly Sheriff, he makes little pay, works long hours and has to share his bed with his wife and a dog. It's a great life living in the country with the bugs and rain. But Dave and Sarah are my friends and I wish I had met Sarah before this big lug did. So raise your glasses and salute the newlyweds."

The reception went on as Dave went around saying hello to people he remembered from his brief stay in Vegas the last time. Sarah was busy gossiping with Penny and Lois, as Jim sat with Deacon, Lynn and Greg Warren.

"So Greg, any more word on Hallson?" Jim asked.

"His written confession was an eye-opener. He figured that he would be caught eventually, so he wrote the thing to cover his butt. Seems Boering had engineered the whole thing to get some glory for catching the bad guys, which was supposed to be Manny Finnerman, the fall guy. But Hallson killed Finnerman because he jeopardized the plot. Hallson felt bad that so many people were killed by the sunblock, he said Boering told him it would just make people sick. He was going to skip town to get away from Boering, but he didn't know Boering would kill him. So it's all tied up and done."

"Good thing for you he did write that confession. Feel good about being back?"

"Yep, and Weber said he was putting me in to fill the vacant Lieutenant slot." Warren said with a grin.

"Very good, you deserve it, Greg," Lynn said.

Around eleven the party had wound down and Deacon told Jim he would drive Stevens, Lois and Virgil back to the hotel. They all left and Jim went to Dave standing by himself waiting for Sarah to say goodbye to people.

Dave told Jim that he and his new bride were going back to the guesthouse. "And we don't want to be disturbed," he warned.

"We won't bother you guys. Do you want us to take Van Gogh for the night so you won't be disturbed by him on your honeymoon? I'm sure Willy would love to have a playmate for a sleep over."

"Sure, that's sounds great. You can come and get him before you retire for the night. Good luck sleeping with him around," Dave said with a laugh.

Jim asked Fred to drive them to the guesthouse and he could return the limo in the morning. Fred smiled and said it would be at the office.

On the way driving home, Penny sighed loudly. "This was a great week, despite your crime. I had so much fun with Sarah and even Lois. She's a strange woman, but nice."

"Now what? We're done with the wedding, everyone is going back to Washington tomorrow. I think we had talked about going on a long vacation."

"I talked to Gordy at the reception and told him I may want to get away for a while. Do you think Dave and Sarah could put up with us for a short visit?"

"Dave told me he expected us to come up. Maybe we'll wait a week or two before we go visit. Or we could get in the motorhome and just drive, not knowing where we were going."

"That sounds adventurous. As much as I love Sarah, I think I need a rest from her. She's so energetic, it makes me tired," Penny said with a laugh.

"We'll talk about it tomorrow."

Early the next morning, Jim was covered by dogs. Willy was on his chest and Van Gogh was across his legs. "Great, I'm trapped," he said and struggled to move the huge Airedale off his legs.

Penny was already up, so Jim went to his bathroom and got ready for the day, followed by Willy and Van Gogh.

He came out to the kitchen to find Penny, Dave and Sarah all having coffee.

"Good morning, Jim," Dave said. "We've packed the car and are itching to drive back home. Not that we didn't enjoy your company, but we miss home."

"I wish you woke me earlier, I would have helped to get you out of here. I'm tired of the both of you," Jim laughed.

Sarah stood and gave Jim a kiss on the cheek. "We feel the same way, dear. Too much crime and too many murders down here. We're ready to go back to where we have only serial killers and terrorists. Simple crimes like that."

They all went out to Dave's car and said their goodbyes. Jim and Penny watched them drive off. "Now we have to get the rest of the clan out of town. Shall we go take everyone to the airport?" Jim asked.

"Yes, then we will come back and have our own little honeymoon."

"I like the way you think," Jim said with a slap to Penny's butt.

"Hey, don't start so soon, let's get our guests on their way."

They turned to go back into the house, when Jim's cell phone buzzed.

"If you answer that, I'll divorce you. No more crimes," Penny warned him.

"Yes, dear," Jim said, and they went in the house.

THE END

Jim Richards Family of Readers

Thanks to the following people who are now part of the Jim Richards Family of Readers. They have read a book or more and enjoyed them. They all volunteered to be included in the list. If you are a fan of the books, send me your full name and you will be included in future books. Send your name to murdernovels@bobmoats.com to be added here and on the website.

* Achim Feifel * Al Norris * Alex Wheatley * Alexandra Delporte-Wilkinson * Amy Tapia * Andrea Bryan * Anne Shepherd * Arianda Sugar * Arlene Markowski * Ashley Augustus * Audra Hall * Barbara Hughes * Barbara Sammons * Barbara Schuler * Barbara Zirger * Beth Donohue Plenskofski * Beth Rosin * Betsy Childress * Beth Gibson * Bill Sandy * Bill Tornquist * Billie-jo Collie * Boni J Rychener * Candace Larson * Carl Bishopric * Carla Lewis * Carole Henderson * Carolyn Conroy * Carolyn Riddle-Linington * Cassy Bailey * Cathie Turner * Chad Hudson * Charlie Meier * Charlotte L Duran * Cheryl L. Everett * Cindy Ackley Nunn * Cindy Valstad * Connie Bancroft * Corinne Kay O'Daniel * Dana Robbins Chuchran * Dana Wichita * Daniel Kalus * Danielle Monique * Darren Heald * Dave Travers * David Wilkinson * DeAnn Jannereth * Deanna Miller * Deb Breuker Balbo * Debbie Carter * Debbie White * Deborah Fartuch * Deborah Gauze * Deborah Sullivan * Dee King * Denise Freeman * Diana Carver * Dixie Beck * Donna Gould * Donna Thompson * Donny Minter * Doris Kight * Eddie Moore * Eric Walters * Felicia Annette Bradfield * Francine Menor * Gail Chesney *

Toxic Murders

Georgiann Minster * George Conner * Greg Colucci * Hayley Rankin * Harold Garcia * Heidi Arnold * Irma Ranee Coy * Jack Plunkitt * Jacqueline Moss * Jan Kimball * Jane Lawson * Janice Schneider * Janice Spoor * Jennifer Besner * Jennifer Redmond * Jerry Dornak * Jessica Keown-Belous * Jim Beck * Jo Boguslaw * Jo Turner * Joan Kimball * Joanne Marie Turner * John Peiffer * John Wisbiski * Joseph Wauro * Joyce Stacy * Joyce Trifiletti * Judy Franklin * Judy Travers * Judy Padgett * Julie Heath * Junnahvee Benson * Karen Dahl * Karen Grams * Karen Higham * Karen Kaiser * Karen Meinburg Richwine * Karen Kirkman Parker * Karin Hawkins * Karin Vasvari * Kathleen Donohue Roesing * Kathleen Riddle-Wolfe * Kathy Hinds Moore * Kathy Jones * Kathy Mitchell * Katie Benzler * Kay Burns * Kelly Garcia * Ken Boggs * Keota Rodriguez * Kiera Mccarthy * Kim Estes * Kimberley May * Kitty Stolle * Kristie Sciler * Kirsty Stanton * LaLonnie Scallen * Larry Morris * Leann Parr * Lenora Scales * Leslie Marie Jackson * Linda Forester * Linda Ingle Cox * Linda Kennerö * Linda Magill * Lisa Bower * Lisa Keller * Liz Gibson * Lorraine Wiman * Loretta Alexander * Lynda Bowles * Lynette Lawrance * LuAnn Louttit * Mandy Nutt * Manny Rothman * Marcia Gibson DeWitt * Marie Calder * Marlene Bryan * Mary Hauser * MaryLouise Kramp * Mary Lynn Gross * Megan Atkins * Meghan Hyden * Melody Cannavan * Michael Carruthers * Michael Dinkens * Michael Vannoy * Michelle Burns-Mitchell * Michelle Pilcher * Micki Potter * Mike Moats * Mimi Baur * Myrna Hecht * Nadine Sutton * Nancy Ellen Sayre * Natalie Quine * Neena Martin * O'Della Wilson * Pat Pollington * Pat Rohn * Patricia Jarmon * Patricia C Trezza * Patrick Barry * Paul Lawrance * Peggy Davis * Phyllis Bassett * Raylene Matheny * Rebecca Collins Besner * Renee Brumley * Reta Hanna *

Reta Moats * Robert Lenski * Roberta Navarro-Harder * Sally Berneathy * Sally Hubler * Sarah Santos * Satka Nikc * Sharon E. Edwards * Sharon Mangini * Sharon McMillon * Sheena Rawl * Sherry Amstutz * Shirley Alvarez * Shirley Davies * Shirley Williams * Stacie Rowe * Stephanie Conner * Steve Cullen * Susan Haughton * Susan Hesse Adams * Susan Salomon * Suzan K Chase * Suzanne B. Bryere * Taisha Cullum * Tamara Moore * Tammy Castleberry * Tammy Lynn Wood * Ted Murphy * Terri Atkins * Terri Creech * Terry Raab * Tonia Rachael Riggs-Williams * Tonya Mann * Travis Fleury-Lopez * Twyla Gawlas * Val Brooks * Walt Munsel * Yvonne Isakson *

Thank you to all these wonderful people.

Thank you for purchasing this book. I hope you enjoy it as much as I enjoyed writing it for my faithful readers. Please feel free to email me to tell me what you thought about my stories. I love hearing from the readers. I can be reached at murdernovels@bobmoats.com thanks again!

*

www.ingramcontent.com/pod-product-compliance
Lightning Source LLC
Chambersburg PA
CBHW070823120626
46556CB00002B/633